THE PROPOSING KIND

BREW HA HA #4

BRIA QUINLAN

THE BREW HA HA BOOKS

The Last Single Girl

Worth the Fall

The Catching Kind

The Proposing Kind

FREE prequel short story: It's In His Kiss

Sign-up for the New Release Alerts HERE

Welcome to The Proposing Kind! If you haven't read The Catching Kind, you probably want to do that first because this is the reader-requested sequel. Plus, The Catching Kind is really funny. My mom and both her cats will tell you it is, so it must be true.

Don't want to go read it? Well, pre-readers say you really should read it, but if you're going to be all *I Don't Need No Stinking First Book*, here's what you need to know in super fast points:

Hailey Tate is a YA writer who gets matched up by her agent with Connor Ryan, America's Sexiest Athlete (and playboy). Of course, Connor and Hailey had a bit of a scuffle right before this happens. Connor dismisses her as beneath his notice as he hits on a model. Hailey dismisses him as beneath her notice because... well, can he even read?

Obviously neither of them wants anything to do with the other—only, if they don't pretend for the public to be the next celebrity couple, both their agents have threatened Bad Things will happen (Hailey moves to Connor's agency and Connor loses a promotional deal and perhaps his spot on the Nighthawks).

So, they become the fake couple of the century. Hainnor? Conley? Something.

Hijinks, hilarity, and hearts are involved.

There is an argument about a dog they don't own.

The paparazzi gets involved and Hailey is Just. Not. Ready for that stuff to get real.

When it's time to part, Hailey knows she's let the worst possible thing happen—she's fallen in love with Connor.

Of course they end up together, but readers wanted more. And so here is that more.

Happy reading!

ONE

"Hails!" Connor shouted from the kitchen. The kitchen where my nice warm bed wasn't. "Hailey!"

I dragged a pillow over my head. He had more than enough caffeine in there to get him through whatever was going through his overactive mind—*the addict*. There was no way I was getting up at...I rolled over and looked at the clock. Seriously? Four forty-eight in the morning?

"Hailey!" Connor stood in the doorway, a pair of track pants hanging off his hips, a steaming cup of coffee wrapped in his oversized mitt of a hand. "Gavin is in South America."

Okay. I knew I wasn't awake yet, but I wasn't sure what Gavin's travels had to do with anything.

"Why?"

"Something about work and hang gliding. Which," he raged on as he stomped to the dresser and set the coffee down before pacing my tiny room. "He went *hang gliding*. Hang gliding. Without me."

"You're not allowed to go hang gliding." Which honestly, with the ideas he and his brother came up with, I was more than a little glad the team owners had rules about what Connor was and wasn't allowed to do to put his body at risk.

"Like he couldn't have waited a few more years." He crossed his arms, and I'm not gonna lie. I was momentarily distracted by the perfectly sculpted upper body that somehow came attached to my pro-athlete boyfriend. "Hails. My eyes are up here."

"Right...but the prettier part of you is a bit lower."

"Hailey Tate." He sounded way more insulted than I'd expected...which was not at all. "My eyes are stunning. *People Magazine* said so."

Of course they did.

"Well, if *People* said so, who am I to argue?"

"Right. So, Gavin." He took another sip of coffee. "Gavin has taken off to South America and I need him. I need to talk to him about something. Important stuff."

"Well, call him." So I can go back to sleep.

Part of me wondered if I'd said the second part out loud based on the look he gave me.

"I can't. No reception wherever he is." He paced the room again, back and forth. Back and forth. "Here's the thing. I think I need to marry you."

I—

Um...

What?

I tried to say words. I'm not sure what they were going to be, but it didn't really matter because after a moment, Connor just carried on.

"If Gavin was here, I'd take him out for a beer—"

"At four-something in the morning?" I asked, oddly stuck on the wrong thing.

"No." Connor looked at me as if *I'd* lost my mind. But I didn't wake him up to announce that I had an obligation to marry him. "Tonight."

"Then would I still be asleep if Gavin were here?"

"Maybe." He ran a gaze down my leg to where my toes stuck out from the bottom of the blanket and smirked. "Maybe not."

I tried not to get sidetracked by the look he gave me. Especially since he may or may not have just proposed.

"Connor..." I waved my hand at him, hoping he'd keep talking long enough for my brain to catch up.

"Right. So, Gavin is gone and I feel like I need to propose to you and since my brother-slash-best friend is gone, I need to talk it out with my other best friend."

"Okay." I nodded, not really sure what all this meant.

"You, Hailey! You're my other best friend." He rolled his eyes at me.

I was pretty sure I was going to have to uninvite him to the rest of my book signings if he was just going to pick up the bad habits of some of my tween readers.

"Oh, that's so sweet." I pushed the blankets down and crawled to the end of the bed to give him a hug. "You're my other best friend too."

Connor snorted. "Right, after Jenna, Kasey, Jayne, Max, and...Dane."

He spit Dane's name out as if it was a curse he wasn't allowed to say in the house. He was still a little bitter about Dane supposedly planning on marrying me once he was done sleeping with every available woman under forty.

"No, sweetie. Just Jenna and Kasey. And really," I gave him a quick squeeze, "when you think about it, they're more like one person. So you have Gavin and I have Jensey...um, Kasna. Something."

"You're just saying that to make me feel better." Connor rested his cheek on top of my head, melting into my hug.

He was still struggling with closing the gap between who he was in real life and who he let the other Nighthawks see. We'd been hanging out with his teammate Marcus and his wife, Chantelle, a bit and it had been really good to see Connor around a guy who didn't want to arrest him or hit him for dating me.

Ah, the small joys.

"I'm not," I answered. And it was true. "You're my favorite person for a lot of things. And trust me, you're glad you aren't that person for things like pedicures and PMS talk."

His back muscles under my hands tightened. Sadly, even big strong pro-baseball players panicked at those three little letters.

"So..." How to reenter this conversation? "Why do you think you *have* to marry me?"

Connor's hand slipped down my back, running his fingers along the length of my spine and back up. Up and down. I was still trying to figure out if he did that at times like this to calm me down or himself.

"Well, I like your place better than mine."

"Which explains why you're always here." I hid my grin in his shoulder. "Plus, even if you lived here, that leather chair is still mine."

He made a low *mm-hmm* sound and kept going. "And, I want to be around you all the time."

Well, that was sweeter.

"And, if we're married, the paparazzi would leave you alone after the initial ridiculousness around whatever dress you wore and if you did something fancy with your hair. I think you'd feel safer without them following you everywhere."

Okay, still sweet, but not exactly romantic. In Connor's brain, that was probably right up there with roses though.

"And," he rushed on, "I'm in love with you and don't want any other guy to even look at you. Unless he's looking at you because he realizes you're with me and he can admire from a distance. And also so no matter what we're always together. And so we can get a dog."

And with that mysterious flow of thought from my otherwise intelligent boyfriend, he pulled back, kissed me on the nose, and turned away.

A gut-deep sigh rushed out of him as if just saying all that took the pressure off.

"Okay. Thanks." He pulled a t-shirt over his head and headed for the door, high-fiving me as he went. "Good talk. Off to the trainers."

I sat on the edge of the bed, staring at the hand I'd somehow auto-offered for the high-five, trying to figure out what in the world had just happened as the door fell shut behind him.

TWO

After the door fell shut behind Connor, my brain caught up with his announcement.

And my heart caught up with my brain a moment later, kicking into a double-time panic pace.

Since it was too early for an emergency margarita meeting, I texted the girls to meet me at The Brew. Caffeine would have to be my drink of choice this time. I was leaning on the doorframe, waiting for the café to open, when Abby jerked the door open from inside.

She stepped aside, letting me nearly fall on my rear. I was moving almost as gracefully as Kasey when I'd brought her to the gym...which will never, ever happen again. The gym manager said their insurance wasn't good enough for her to even walk by the front of the building.

"Since when do you show up here before six a.m.?" Abby looked at me, waiting more patiently than normal for an answer before ushering me.

"Since this is an emergency." I glanced around, trying to put a complete thought together. "I'll have...I'll have coffee."

"You hate coffee." Abby stated this as fact.

"Do I? Do I hate coffee?" I demanded. Maybe I loved coffee. All those stressed-out people drank coffee. Maybe they drank it because of the stress.

"Yes. You hate coffee. How about a nice mug of steamed milk with a little shot of hazelnut and a chocolate muffin that's just coming out of the oven?"

I glared at the girl, confused about what was going on and why she was being so nice. The humoring level was ridiculously high for Abby unless there was some sick and twisted steamed-milk punch line coming.

"Who are you and what have you done with Abby?"

"It's early and I haven't maxed on stupidity yet." Abby shoved the door shut and threw the lock behind her. "Don't make me regret this."

"Okay." I followed her toward the counter but she pointed at the chairs on the other side of the room.

"Don't cramp my style. I'm baking here." She started toward the kitchen then stopped. "Can you build a fire?"

"Um. You mean, like rub two sticks together and...POOF. Fire?"

Abby stood, arms crossed, staring me down. "Remember what I just said about not making me regret this?"

"Right. Yeah."

I glanced toward the fireplace. How hard could it be? Then I remembered it involved fire and that The Brew was one of my favorite places in the world.

After a moment, I caved. "I...um, I doubt I'm fire-competent."

She shook her head and swerved back toward the fireplace next to our chairs.

"Just light the paper sticking out from under those logs. Just the paper. Not the wood...or your hair. Or anything else. Especially not the new rug. I basically have to blackmail John to update anything that's been here for seven bazillion years already."

She gave me a very clear look that said she doubted I could handle this before moving on to take care of what I could only assume were the amazing smells coming from the kitchen.

Following her ever so clear directions, I lit the paper then turned my overstuffed chair to face the fire, watching it because, with Abby as the boss of me, fire failure was not an option.

"Here." A steaming mug was shoved under my nose. "Drink this."

Before I could say thanks, she was gone again.

Oh, the mysterious ways that were Abby.

I sat there, gazing at the fire, drinking my oddly comforting milk thing and wondering if I was engaged or not.

I mean, knowing Connor it's not like he'd *expect* me to say no...or yes. He'd just state we were getting married and be done with it. No one would be surprised.

He'd probably just call his people—who he had decided were also *my* people—and BAM. Sneak-attack wedding. I'd never see it coming.

Luckily handfasting was no longer valid and legal.

Not that I Googled it or anything...and then got distracted by pictures of Jaime—I mean, Sam Heughan.

"So?" Abby sat down, crossed one oversized Mary Jane over the other, and gave me her typical *What have you crazy kids gone and done now* look.

"What?" I asked, because did I really want to be beholden to Abby?

She rolled her eyes so dramatically I thought she might make herself pass out. There was definitely an eye-rolling epidemic going on around here.

"So why are you here at the crack of dawn, drinking comfort milk, and waiting for your girls to show up?" She leaned forward, her eyes narrowing. "Did Muffin Guy dump you?"

"Muffin Guy?" Of all the things she could have nicknamed Connor, that hadn't even crossed my mind.

"It's not every guy who will get up early to use his complete lack of baking skills to make you a muffin." She went on to defend him before I could let her know that, no, I hadn't been dumped. And he was adorable when he attempted to bake for me.

This was true. If only the world knew.

Scratch that.

The last thing I needed was women thinking Connor was hotter.

Except maybe Connor thinking Connor was hotter.

"Well?" Abby wasn't exactly one to let things go.

"He...he might have—"

A pounding on the window cut me off mid-sentence. Jenna, Kasey, and Jayne stood outside shivering in the fluffy, light snow drifting down and painting their coats white.

"I suppose you want me to let them in." Abby glanced toward the door. "It's kind of nice with just one of you. Maybe we could limit the number of people allowed in at a time."

"You do. It's called a fire ordinance and I'm pretty sure it's more than one."

"Yeah. Well, a girl can dream." She pushed herself out of the overstuffed chair and wandered over to the door, completely ignoring the fact that it was freezing outside. Cracking it open just enough to speak to my friends, she went on, "You all want to come in now too?"

Kasey gave the door a little push and strolled in, Jayne shaking her head and following.

"Don't think that just because I made her comfort milk you guys get some too." Abby crossed back over and sat down on the loveseat like she belonged there.

The girls hovered, staring at her before glancing to me and back again. I shrugged. It wasn't like she wouldn't ferret out what was going on and chime in anyway.

She might as well do it in real time.

"So, ladies, you're here because he dumped her." Abby shook her head like this was a tragedy, but one she believed.

"He *dumped* you?" Jenna's eyes went round behind her glasses. Of course this would shock her. She had all of our lives mapped out to happiness and mine was contingent on Connor and the happy couple gene she was sure we shared. "Seriously?"

"No. Not seriously." I shook my head and rolled my eyes at Abby, glad to give it back to her for once.

"Really?" Abby sounded more surprised than anything. "Well, that's good. I was afraid he was being a complete idiot."

I stared at her, a bit shocked by the vehemence ripping the edges of her tone. "That is probably the sweetest thing you've ever said to me."

Abby shook her head. "Don't get used to it."

Of course not.

Dangerous territory. Like a spider with a web, dragging you in with silky, invisible threads of kindness.

"So, Connor didn't dump you," Jenna hedged. "But there's an emergency?"

I glanced from girl to girl, realizing I'd gotten them out of the house hours before most of our careers had us out of bed...hours after most of us had just *gone* to bed, and suddenly felt stupid.

"He, umm..." Maybe I could pretend this was a surprise party for something. Nothing really came to mind though. "Umm..."

"Okay, why don't we do this one question at a time?" Jayne patted my knee then leaned back in her chair giving me space. "Is this about Connor?"

I nodded. That was easy.

"Good. Nice." She smiled encouragingly. "Did something bad happen?"

I stared at her, struggling to define bad.

"All right," Jayne nodded like it was okay. "Maybe *bad* is too broad. Obviously something sent you into emergency mode. Let's back it up. Did Connor do anything on the breakup list?"

I tried to shake my head, but then realized I had no idea what that was. "What's the breakup list?"

"You know. The breakup list." Jayne glanced around the circle, obviously frustrated when everyone, including Abby, shook their heads. "The list of reasons you'd break up with a guy."

"You made a list?" Kasey sounded a bit worried as she asked. "When exactly did you make this list?"

"Um, always." Jayne looked around. "You guys don't make breakup lists?"

"Are they different for every guy?" Jenna reached in her bag, trying to very subtly pull out her always-present notebook. "Is there like a master list and each guy gets say...seven added for him?"

"Why seven?" Abby looked at Jenna like she'd lost her mind. "Why not two or forty?"

"Well, forty seems excessive."

"For the love of color swatches everywhere! A *list of reasons to break up* with someone seems excessive." Kasey stared at Jayne as if she'd never seen her before, a friend of a decade, and chewed at her bottom lip.

"Getting back to the list..." I hedged because this was far more interesting than whether or not I was engaged. Or at least that's what I was telling myself.

Jayne shrugged, obviously knowing this group too well to try to dodge the question.

"You know, every guy is different. You have the standard ones such as if he cheats on me. Then with other guys you'd have things more specific to them, like if he works too much. Etcetera, etcetera." She rolled her hand in front of her as if that explained it all.

Everyone stared at her, not quite sure what to say. Okay, not everyone.

"What if the guy works too much, but that wasn't on the list?" Oh, nice question. Score one for Abby.

"He gets a pass for a while. Then you address it. Then you address it again. Then you add it to the list." Jayne counted each progressive item off on her fingers as she went.

"So basically, what you're saying is everything is on the list?" Kasey gave her A Look. I was really glad Jayne was taking the hit on girlfriend-judgment today. Especially since no one had had caffeine yet.

"No. Just a couple things." She was starting to sound a bit defensive, as if finally realizing no one else thought this was completely normal.

"But," Kasey pushed, "everything has the ability to end up on the list at any time?"

"Of course."

"And," Kasey pushed on, "do you take something off when you add something? Is there a limit? Does the guy suddenly get a pass on something else? Do bad things come off if he hasn't done them in a while? Like getting off probation?"

"Are you saying that dating me is like a prison sentence?" Jayne asked, her voice dropping dangerously.

"Well, I hadn't been..." Kasey stated, leaving a door wide open.

We all watched Kasey, waiting for her to extrapolate.

"You know what?" Jenna stood up. "I could use some caffeine

to help with translating all this craziness. Maybe Abby could do our orders early—" She raised her hand to stop Abby's protest. "We'll wait for you to come back to dive into everyone's insanity. And when you're back, we'll start with Hailey's bat signal."

Everyone's gaze slipped my way. I shouldn't have wanted off the hook. I was the one who called them all in a panic. But now that they were here, I didn't know how to do this without making myself look like an idiot. Or Connor.

I loved my friends, but I sometimes felt like they were still all waiting for a reason to hate him. It made me especially protective, not only of him but of our relationship.

Abby headed toward the counter without taking our orders, and started blending and mixing things at a faster than normal pace. Apparently everyone was interested in the current love life messes we each were building.

No one pushed while Abby was gone—probably partially because she threatened to withhold their caffeine indefinitely if they did.

I closed my eyes, resting my head back against the overstuffed cushion behind me and replaying the morning. It was typical Connor. He was both impulsive and strategic. I suddenly wondered how many insane ideas he talked himself out of with Gavin as his sounding board.

Maybe that's all this was. Maybe he thought marrying me was an insane idea. Maybe the whole *good talk* thing was because he'd gotten the idea out of his system and moved on.

What if—

"Hurry up, Abby!" Jayne stood and rushed over to help her bring all the drinks in one run. "I can see the panic setting in."

Jayne and Abby handed out the drinks and sat down, everyone looking at me expectantly as if I was just going to dive into the point.

"I might be engaged!" Okay, so I was going to dive right into the point.

You'd think an announcement like that would merit some type of reaction.

Wait for it...wait for it...wait for—

Or, not.

"Did you hear me?" I asked, glancing around the circle. "I said, I might be engaged."

"Huh." Jenna gave me one of those smiles that lulled you into thinking she was completely innocent. "So, I might be congratulating you...right?"

I sighed, dropping back in my chair and closing my eyes again before gathering my already annihilated wits and glaring at each friend in turn. Then I glared at Abby, because if she wanted in on this she deserved a little glaring too.

"You guys really fail at morning emergency meetings. If it's before the alarm clock or there's no alcohol involved, a girl just can't count on you." I glanced around the room, trying to figure out why people weren't telling me what to do. These women *excelled* at being opinionated. Especially... "Abby. Seriously. Et tu? No opinion?"

Abby shrugged and pulled her phone out, frowned at it, and put it away.

"I have to admit, I'm afraid I'm delusional from the lack of caffeine and the obscene hour my phone started chirping. But," Kasey glanced around the others, obviously trying to garnish support, "I'm not sure how you can *maybe* be engaged."

"Also, honey, do you *want* to be engaged?" Jenna smiled at me, all soft and stuff, but the question hit me in the gut like a fastball.

"Why wouldn't I want to be engaged?"

"You mean to Connor, right?" Abby asked. Why exactly was

Abby here? I mean, besides that she worked here and was suppos-edly supposed to ensure our café needs were met?

"Yes." I tried not to shout, but this wasn't going how it was supposed to go. A girl has engagement—even maybe-engagement—expectations. "To Connor. What is wrong with you guys?"

As they all glanced away, not meeting my eye and for once locking me out of our typical communication circle, I began to panic.

More than when Connor woke up and went insane this morning.

"Guys, come on?" I laughed, trying to lighten up the mood. "What's with all the worry-shmorry?"

"It's just..." Jenna's gaze swept around the group before she powered on. "Well, you've only been together a couple months and Connor doesn't have the best reputation. I guess we just all thought you'd test these waters a bit more."

I collapsed back in my seat, every muscle in my body wilting into mush.

All this time I'd thought they'd forgiven Connor for how things started with us. I mean, they were the ones who encour-aged me to be more open-minded. To let go of the stupidity we both showed when we met.

Now I find out none of them thought we'd make it.

I studied the group, pity coming through each face at their agreement with Jenna, until I got to Abby. She looked...thoughtful.

"What about you?" I tossed a decorative pillow at her when she continued to gaze off into the nothingness. "Ms. Truth Speaker, what do you think?"

Abby shook her head as if clearing it then glared around in her typical unsubtle manner.

"I think you all have a lot of drama in your life for people who don't actually do anything dramatic." She stood, brushing away imaginary crumbs on her apron. "I think I was right about limiting how many of you are allowed in the café at a time."

With that, she stormed her way around the counter and through the doorway to the backroom.

And that is how an a.m. bat signal turned into an emotional butt-whooping.

THREE

When our breakfast meeting didn't get any better, I headed out to the gym to pound the snot out of something.

I left in a flurry of *Don't worry*s and *I'm sure it will all work out*. But not one tone of excitement or joy.

This wasn't how I pictured getting engaged...or maybe-engaged.

I wasn't one of those girls to sit around planning my wedding, but the idea that the man I love might actually want to marry me, a man who could almost literally have any woman he wanted, and my girlfriends' reaction was all, "Oh, yeah. Okay. Um..."

Well, it more than stung.

Luckily, when I called ahead to the gym to reserve a fitness room, there was actually an opening. Maybe I could sneak in without my insane trainer spotting me, enjoy a little pro-health therapy, and sneak back out.

"Hailey!"

Or not.

"Shawn, what's up?" I gave him my most casual smile, pulling my gym bag up on my shoulder and trying to power through the lobby before more questions were asked.

"Looking for a workout?" He grinned. He was always grinning. He managed to be the nicest taskmaster on the planet. There was a chance that he and Jenna were separated at birth.

"Nope. I'm just going to grab a mat and do some weights and—"

"Hailey." He gave me A Look. Again, Shawn. Jenna. Separated at birth theory. "You called ahead to reserve a room with a speed bag. I know you better than that."

"Right. So...I'm just going to go get to it."

I headed through the lobby, flashing my pass at the girl at the front desk as I went by.

I tossed my bag into the corner of the workout room, grabbing my yoga mat and spreading it out in front of the mirror. Before I could even get into a nice, ahhhhh-inducing stretch, Shawn showed up in the doorway.

"Hailey, you're not going to leave me hanging like this?" Shawn grinned at me, a look I was all too familiar with. Usually it made me nervous, but today I needed to have my butt kicked. "Did you really think you could come in here, looking like that, and you wouldn't be working out with me?"

I had no idea what he meant by that. But I was a (reasonably) mature adult and would let that go.

Okay. Maybe not. "What do you mean looking like this?"

"I mean, that." Shawn waved his hand around between us kind of gesturing to me. "Like Hailey, but a very dangerous Hailey who could take out a small nation just by waving her finger at them."

I guess I don't have the whole shake-it-off thing going on.

"Shawn, my friend, if I could take out a small nation with one finger imagine what I could do to you right now."

Unfortunately, my false bravado didn't scare the man off.

Probably because he taught me everything I knew. Of course, none of that included destroying small countries, so everyone was safe.

But, like a good trainer does, he beat me up for the next hour. I worked muscles I hadn't known I had. He'd obviously been leaving those muscles top secret for a bad day. Which means who knows what he had in store for a really, *really* bad day.

As he finished abusing my body, I dropped down on my mat, looking forward to a nice, long stretch to cool down.

"So," Shawn dove right in, no longer keeping us both focused on everything so tightly since the major part of the workout was done. "Are you going to tell me what's going on?"

I glanced at him, doubting I'd get any further sympathy from my male trainer than from my female best friends. But, who knows? Maybe a guy's point-of-view was what I needed.

I opened my mouth to spill it and realized how much dating Connor Ryan—one of the most famous athletes in the country—meant protecting my privacy for more reasons than just my own sanity.

Shawn squatted down next to where I was stretching my quads, back to the door.

"Listen. I know that things are different for you now. That you have to guard your back—and your boyfriend's back—and that there are some people..." he gave a discreet cough and nodded his head toward where the front desk would be on the other side of the gym, "who would take advantage of you. But I'm not one of them. We've been together a long time. I hope you could count me as a safe place. Like a bartender of fitness."

I laughed as he smiled over that, clearly liking the analogy.

I took a deep breath. The thing about Shawn was he's my trainer. He liked Connor, but he was *my* trainer. And, he'd never been judge'y about our relationship.

"Okay." I took a deep breath. "Connor pulled the oddest

thing I've ever seen a guy do this morning and it kind of freaked me out."

Shawn looked at me like he wasn't sure what to say. And who could blame him?

"I didn't really see it coming," I continued. "I mean, he just woke me up and sprung it on me. This isn't the type of thing you spring on a girl."

"In the bedroom?" Shawn asked, looking at me like he wanted to back out of the room.

"Well, yes. But I don't see what room we were in as having anything to do with how weird it is."

He choked, looking toward the door as if he needed help or wanted to escape. "Well, no I guess it wouldn't. But..."

"Also, it was kind of weird because I didn't know if he was serious or not."

"That would make a difference." Shawn slumped against the wall and slid down it, letting his legs stretch out next to me.

"And so, he just put it out there and then high-fived me and left... I'm not sure if I should even address it when I see him later."

"He high-fived you?" Shawn sat up, looking confused. "He suggested whatever it is he suggested, then high-fived you and left?"

"Yes. Right? Weird."

"So...I take it... Hailey, maybe you should just tell me what he suggested." He mumbled something under his breath I was pretty sure was *Not that I really want to know*. But he'd started this, so he was on the hook.

"He said he thought maybe he should ask me to marry him." It sounded just as confusing now as it had with Connor and then later at The Brew.

Shawn sat up, looking at me as if I'd changed the subject. "He asked you to marry him?"

"No. He said he was thinking that *maybe* he *should* ask me to marry him, then basically left."

Shawn studied me. Then he looked off into the distance. Then back at me. Then he shook his head.

"Sorry, Hailey. I got nothing."

"What do you mean you've got nothing?" I could feel the panic rising again. "What happened to being the bartender of fitness?"

"Well, I don't know what his point is. He didn't actually ask so he's just thinking about it. Maybe he wants to ask so he was trying to gauge how reciprocal you'd be to it. I mean, that's a big risk for a guy to just drop to one knee. He's never had to fight for a girl before and now he's thinking about forever with one who won't take his crap. I'm betting you scare the snot out of him."

It never dawned on me that this could be Connor's freak out, not mine.

Okay.

All right.

Okay.

I stood, brushing my hands off and rolling my mat up.

"Thanks, Shawn. That actually helped."

Kind of.

He smiled and waved, looking more relieved than I felt as I wandered out the door.

FOUR

I was almost done with surprises when I got home from the gym. Luckily Shawn had kicked my butt, letting me burn off some of the frustrated confusion I'd been carrying around all morning, and gave me a bit of insight into the male mind.

Or as much as any woman was ever going to get.

I started home, happy to be headed to a place of comfort and consistency. I planned to spend the afternoon brushing off Connor's guy moment and just enjoying working on my next series...or something that could become my new series.

Of course, I couldn't have foreseen the construction going on at my building.

Actually, yes. I *should* have known about construction going on. Unless there'd been structural damage that needed emergency repairs there should have been meetings and notices.

I stood back, watching guys in bright vests and safety helmets measure different parts of our entryway. As I watched, they eventually realized I was behind them and stepped back, waving me through.

It's always interesting when guys in safety gear have no problem letting a girl in sneakers wander through a work zone.

"Is something wrong?" I glanced at the entry's frame, looking for cracks or other damage.

The biggest guy slapped his clipboard against his thigh and glanced down at me, apparently confused—and a bit annoyed— by the question. "Nope."

Wow. Thanks for your clarity.

"So, what's going on?"

I wanted at least the basics of the story before I tracked down Marjory, the president of our condo association, and asked why work was going on without a vote or notification. Marjory thought she was the dictator of a small country not a volunteer for a small HOA. And you'd think the info was confidential the way the guys kept working without giving me anything else to go on.

Finally, when he saw that I wasn't going anywhere, one of the guys stopped to answer. "We're pulling the entryway forward and putting double doors on them." He didn't glance my way again.

I closed my eyes and decided this was not the day I wanted to deal with my HOA money being wasted.

But, tomorrow? Tomorrow I would definitely be dealing with this stuff because I had absolutely no money to waste since I was between contracts.

I stomped up the stairs to my little tiny condo, ready to crash since I'd been up since what is technically the middle of the night...and no, the clock police couldn't convince me otherwise.

When I reached my door, there was a little notice half-shoved under it.

"Dear residents: This week we're having some work done on the front of the building. The added foyer will make our building safer and more attractive."

Wow. Talk about the horses already having left the barn.

But Marjory and I were still going to have a talk.

I didn't know what was going on, but I wasn't going to be kept in the dark much longer. I saw a mission coming on.

As soon as I showered and had caffeine and some words in on my new project.

So, maybe tomorrow.

FIVE

The next morning, I woke up to noise—lots of it.

It took me a few moments to remember I now lived in a construction zone instead of the peaceful oasis of a century old brick building with walls thick enough to resist an explosion.

When I'm starting a new series it's hard enough to get into a new world, but when you aren't even sure what the world is, creating it is nearly impossible with all that noise.

Unless I was going to write a YA construction story.

Huh, maybe there was a market for that.

Nope. Probably not.

And, since I really didn't want to deal with the pounding and noise going on outside there was only one real option.

No. Not the library. They don't have caffeine there.

I packed up my work stuff and headed to The Brew, knowing it would be more peaceful in a public café than in my own little office today. As soon as I got there I felt more relaxed than I'd been in my own home for the last couple days with all the change and surprises.

Nothing changed at The Brew. Everything was good. I'd have a chocolate muffin and some tea and sit in my typical comfy chair and—

"Hi! Can I help you?"

I glanced up at some strange girl standing behind the counter.

"Who are you?" Because that didn't sound rude at all.

"Emily." She pointed at the little homemade nametag shaped like a flower she'd pinned to her shirt.

I stood there, waiting for something a bit more. But she continued to smile at me from behind the counter, looking for all the world as if giving her name was enough to explain what she was doing there.

"Where's Abby?" Because I couldn't imagine Abby letting this girl in her domain.

"Ummmm..." The girl glanced toward the kitchen.

I started to get a little nervous. What if someone had been able to overpower Abby and then locked her body in the kitchen. I mean, it would take a small army just to get past the snark, but what if...

"Emily," Abby peeked her head out, "what's going on?"

I looked at her, not tied up and suffering from Café Takeover, and an odd sort of relief swept over me.

"Abby!" I almost rushed to wrap her up in a huge hug. But I was afraid of the death that awaited me down that lane. "What's going on?"

She glanced at the girl and let out a long-suffering sigh.

"Did you get her muffin? She needs the muffin like ASAP." Abby glanced at the pastry display, probably having an exact count of what was there and noting that there was no missing muffin. "And make sure you heat it on low so the edges don't get too crispy."

The girl looked at me a bit panicked. "She didn't order a muffin."

"She didn't order anything," I said, wondering where the panic was coming from. "Abby, *what* is going on?"

Abby glanced at the girl and snapped, "Heat up the muffin and start an iced green tea," before coming around the counter and ushering me toward the overstuffed chairs.

Once she settled in across from my normal seat, she watched the girl over my shoulder, only shaking her head slightly as I heard something glass hit the floor.

"John hired her." I could hear Abby's annoyance ground through every word. "She just showed up this morning."

She said it as if John had found a kitten that was actually a skunk in disguise.

"John?" I glanced around looking for John, but realized the man was smarter than that. He must have sprung her on Abby then hit the road.

"Yes." Obviously Abby was not thrilled about this development.

I hated to be the one to point out that John actually owned The Brew. I wasn't stupid enough to do that. I just kind of waited, looking at her like this was completely a surprise.

"He said I work too much." She huffed this out and rolled her eyes, obviously put out by the idea.

But honestly, as I thought it over, she really did work too much. And this was coming from a writer who loved to work and basically carried a notebook everywhere for emergency work sessions.

Emergency meaning something inspired me and I needed to ignore everything else to fall into my world *right then*.

Abby was here if The Brew was open and she lived upstairs so her going home time seemed to be limited. John probably had a really good point. But that might not be what she was worried about.

"Can you afford fewer hours?"

She waved the questions away with the flick of her hand as she watched Emily doing something at the counter behind me.

"He promoted me to manager and made my salary what I got paid every week anyway."

"Oh." John, that big softy. "That seems like a pretty good deal."

"Yeah." Only she didn't sound thrilled about it.

"How is she?"

"She has no idea what she's doing." Abby sounded so put out by this that I almost laughed.

"Well, it is her first day."

Abby turned her glare on me, but was quickly distracted when the door opened with one of the regular, mid-morning drop-ins.

"Hi!" Emily greeted from the counter, and I gave into temptation to turn around to watch how things went.

The guy stutter-stepped at the new face behind the counter, before his gaze landed on Abby, a bit confused.

Emily stood there, smile frozen in place.

Giving up pretending to be subtle, I swiveled in my chair to more comfortably follow the guy's progress to the counter to order his coffee. All of us watched closely as Emily made the coffee and brought it back to him, ringing him up on the little iPad register John had upgraded to last month.

"Have a great day!"

"Oh for the love of—" Abby mumbled under her breath at the over-perk going on in her new barista. Abby waved the girl over and waited for her to come, cleaning rag in hand, join us. "She's going to make people expect joy, happiness, and kittens when they come in here."

"Well, that wouldn't suck," I accidentally said out loud. "I mean, kittens probably go against health codes, but still."

"No." Abby gave me A Look. "They get the best coffee and

baked goods in the region. We don't want people having absurd expectations." She raised her voice and pointed at Emily. "Tone down the cheer and joy."

Emily just nodded and smiled, probably realizing there was no way she was winning this argument. Apparently John had hired a smart girl.

Abby could only hold up under Emily's unwavering smile for a moment before she broke. "Okay. Go."

Emily sweetened her smile, but as she turned away from Abby I saw the little eye roll she allowed herself.

I think I was going to like this girl.

"So." Abby sipped her tea, glancing around the café and shaking her head. "John thinks I should go to college."

That was...actually a really good idea. Abby was super smart and had apparently aced her GED.

"And...you don't want to go to college?" I knew there was a landmine in this conversation somewhere.

She shrugged, looking indifferent. Which, Abby looking indifferent usually meant she was anything but.

"What would you go to school for?" It seemed like something I should know, but I couldn't even guess.

She leaned to the side, watching Emily disappear into the kitchen.

"I'm doing what I want to do right now."

"Sitting with me, having tea, and obsessing about the new girl and what she's doing in your kitchen?"

The look she gave me...well, the equivalent words weren't coming out of my mouth anytime soon.

"No. Running a café with the freedom to create new baked goods as I see fit."

It never occurred to me that working here would be her dream. But the more I thought about it the more it made sense. She loved to bake, was extremely talented at it, liked to be in charge. And even though John owned the place he was incredibly gifted at letting her think she ran it...even as he hired someone else around her.

"Maybe John thinks you want to run your own...or maybe he just thinks you'd like college."

She dropped her head, giving me a look from under her bangs that said it all. "College students come in here every day. If they're the best and the brightest, I think I'd rather just learn through life."

"Don't forget, in a lot of ways they're also a lot younger than you."

She nodded, magnanimously agreeing that the little people did not have the life experience that it took to circle her sphere.

"Maybe," was all she finally said.

I listened to the banging around in the kitchen and watched Abby's hands tighten on her teacup as she struggled not to go find out what was going on. It was bizarre.

"You know what? I can't take this anymore!" I tried not to wave my hands around since that seemed a little dramatic even for me. "What is going on with all the change?"

Right then Emily set down a tray painted with bright flowers and holding two cups of tea and a chocolate muffin.

I couldn't help but smile at the little addition to our table even as Abby glared at the tray like it was a betrayal of maximum capacity.

"Anything else?" Emily asked with a smile

"Don't ask them that. We don't want them to expect that kind of service."

"But—"

"No."

The girl nodded at Abby then headed back to the counter where she stood like a sentinel watching us.

"Why?" Abby took a sip from her fresh tea, obviously looking for a reason to not like it. "What else is going on? I mean, besides the fact that you don't know if you're engaged or not."

There's the Abby I know and kinda-loved.

"Just...everything. Okay?"

She looked at me like I was making even less sense than normal, so I went with the most distracting topic that came to mind.

"So, college?" That was just one more thing that might change.

"Yeah." She didn't sound thrilled about it. Maybe I wasn't the only one not enjoying all the change.

But then, I wasn't a teenager...or however old Abby was.

"Abby, how old are you?" It dawned on me we all assumed a lot of things about her, but as I'd gotten to know her, even with the amount of snark she managed to toss out, I started to think she couldn't possibly really be seventeen.

Even Abby had to age. I'd seen her in sunlight.

She gave me a look like I'd asked her something really personal. I hadn't thought age was a big secret.

"Twenty-one."

"Really. Huh." That made her only four years younger than me.

"Well, I will be." Abby glanced around for Emily, then lowered her voice. "Thursday."

"It's your birthday!" I loved birthdays. Like woot-woot love'm, bring'em on *Love!*

"Shhhh." Abby shook her head *and* rolled her eyes. This must be a big deal.

"We need to do something." I pulled out my phone and started texting the girls. "We'll go out! Birthday! Wooooo!"

"Okay, so, you're insane. I thought you were the sane one, but I'm questioning that now."

"Don't you want to celebrate?" But then I had a thought.

Abby knew everything about us, but we didn't know that much about her. Some of that was on purpose. We knew she had some type of rough history that was not to be asked about, but beyond that... "I mean, unless you already have plans."

"No." She sounded unsure, as if she might have plans.

"Great!" I went back to texting the girls. Then I texted John to get Abby a night off and ask if his girlfriend, Sarah, wanted to join us. Then I texted Connor to tell him it was Abby's birthday.

I finally glanced up to Abby's sardonically confused look. "Did you reach the Space Station? I'm not sure they know."

My phone started dinging back and I just gave her a look and paged through the responses.

"John will close Friday night. We'll all meet here." I gave her a wink. "Bring your A-game."

"I need to go get some work done." Abby stood, shaking her head at me like I was a weird, new creature, and headed back to dictate the world of Emily.

And with that I headed back to my newly secured condo, afraid of what I'd find after being gone an entire hour.

SIX

I wrapped up my pages for the day, a hard outline with some really great worldbuilding notes and a new creature I had to do some mythological research on. I loved this stuff. These were the days when things felt easy. When the fury of a muse was so great, I was just along for the ride because I was too excited to slow down for anything.

I saved my notes, backed them up, backed them up again, and got up to stretch.

Rolling out my yoga mat—which, contrary to Kasey's beliefs was not for picnicking—I started some warm-up stretches to get the writer-knots moving out of my shoulders and back.

Of course my butt would be straight up in the air when the door opened.

"Hey! Nice greeting." Connor laughed as I heard him drop something by the door.

I rolled my eyes and glared at him over my shoulder. Instead of moving along, he lifted the coffee table up and over me then dropped to the floor to match my stretch.

"How's it going?" he asked, as he exhaled and shifted with me to the next move.

"Good. Today was super productive. I'm almost ready to let my agent know about my new concept." I held the stretch letting my muscles tense then start to relax.

That seemed to be the entire basis of living right now: tense slipping toward relaxed, then handspringing back to tense.

"That's great." Connor was nothing if not supportive of my career.

I think the fact that he also had a career that didn't allow him a lot of flexibility created an understanding that most people didn't have. They thought writing meant "working at home" and that meant napping on the couch watching soaps for six hours then tossing words on the page for twenty minutes.

I glanced toward Connor, watching him flex his way out of the stretch and felt such a deep contentment slide over me that I almost sighed out loud.

I sat up and leaned back on my hands, watching Connor finish the stretch he was easing out of.

He shifted, sitting up as well before crossing his legs to sit on the floor next to me. After a moment he leaned over and brushed a kiss across my lips, giving me the same shudder he'd given me since I'd stopped fighting our attraction.

Sure, half the country was attracted to Connor, but my feelings for him were way stronger than the draw of his pretty face. And, we'd worked hard to earn this after the way our relationship had started—fake and full of animosity. But real and full of love was a lot better.

"So," he leaned over and swept a kiss across my lip so quickly I couldn't even react. "Marcus asked if I wanted to rent a house together in Florida for spring training."

Connor grinned at me like a loon. I was tempted to make a joke about him making a friend—a real friend—but realized it was too important a moment. He'd set aside his need to compete with every human with a Y chromosome and seemed so much happier for it.

"Oh, cool." I liked Marcus. He was happy with his life, settled with his wife, and not a partier.

"We thought that way when you and Chantelle come down, we're not living in one of those houses where the guys are throwing frat boy wannabe keggers every night." He shifted so his hand covered mine where we sat on the floor. "I want you to be comfortable there so you'll be there a lot."

This had been an ongoing theme lately—the Spring Training Separation Period.

I was worried about the separation, but Connor was a wee bit obsessed with it. He'd had his handy-dandy personal assistant, Nick, doing things like printing out flight schedules and marking all flights from New England to Florida in blue with pink for return flights. He'd already asked me what I'd need to work remotely and for how long I felt comfortable not being at my house.

Poor Nick was probably trying to balance his other clients while solving imaginary scenarios that hadn't happened yet so Connor wouldn't worry about them.

"That's sweet." I thought about how often I'd be able to get down there—which was, not that much.

Florida was not a cheap flight time with spring break and people getting sick of the winter. I figured I'd get maybe two trips down.

"I can see your brain working." Connor gave me a grin and eased back, lying on the floor beside me. "Stop. Paying for the travel isn't a big deal for me. It's not like a gift. It's not me paying."

"Um, it would be you paying if you paid." I pointed it out since this seemed like just one more way Connor's logic was slipping.

"Hails, I'm a multimillionaire. If I can't spend my money on the things I want the most—which is time with you when I'm away—then what can I spend it on?" He sounded so sincere that I stretched out next to him, cuddling into his side as he continued. "I've already looked at the schedule and asked Marcus when Chantelle and their daughter typically come down. I know you're on your own schedule too, but we put in long days. You'd have plenty of time to work. I'll have a car down there for you to go wherever you want. You could maybe do some readings and stuff if we can get those scheduled."

I let this run through my mind, considering the schedule as I went. It wasn't a vacation—he was right. I could make this work. And, if this was what the future held, I needed to be able to compromise if I expected him to.

"So, I haven't driven a car in six or seven years," was all I said in reply.

He flashed me that gorgeous, happy smile. "I'll make sure Nick gets us a lot of insurance then."

I dropped my head back down onto his chest and relaxed into him, letting him make lists of things for Nick to do in his head. This was what my life had become—and it was a pretty good life.

This man, this insanely talented, kind-hearted, world famous, chaotic-minded man may have asked me to marry him.

Or maybe he didn't.

SEVEN

I couldn't believe I was going out for Abby's birthday. It was still taking an adjustment to realize she wasn't some snotty teenager. She was actually just a cynical twenty-something.

In retrospect, it wasn't that much of a surprise. She'd been a steady presence in our lives. Her being one of the girls was kind of already an unspoken truth.

"So, you guys are taking Abby out to make her a woman, huh?" Connor lounged in the leather chair, feet propped up on the coffee table.

"You know," I glanced over at him stretched out on my favorite piece of furniture, "if you don't bother to ever go sit in your own chair, it's not going to break in nice and cozy like that one."

"Yeah. That's okay." He gave me a typical over-confident Connor smile, like he knew something I didn't about the chair. *My* chair.

He was probably paying someone to go sit in the new chair at his place every day so it would eventually be broken in exactly how he wanted. Knowing my clever, clever man, he probably interviewed people based on their height, weight, and body mass to make sure the person exactly matched his form.

Probably compared butts and everything.

I just shook my head at him. There was really no sense in trying to comprehend the way Connor's brain worked. With that, I headed into the bedroom to figure out what to wear.

Luckily, I still had Personal Shopper Becca's binder to work with, so it wasn't all that hard. And, since my agent was still feeling bad about the whole blackmailing-me-to-fake-date-a-player, she was still paying for Becca and her magic binder. I just had to open the huge color-coded binder to Girls' Night Out and adjust for weather. And the fact that I didn't want my butt hanging out of anything. Most suggestions were perfect, but for some reason Becca had an addiction to club clothes she kept thinking I'd wear.

Halloween seemed like a good time for that. It's shocking how few Slutty Writer costumes there were for sale.

Unfortunately, girls' night out meant breaking in more shoes. Becca loved shoes more than Carrie Bradshaw. The higher the heel, the better in her world. I, on the other hand, could live in flip-flops, Chucks, and Uggs...weather dependent.

Flipping through the binder, everything seemed flashier than I was looking to wear. I'd have to tell Becca to come up with some slightly more casual going-out clothes for next year. Something with flats. Because, unfortunately, if Connor was here to stay, so was having to look like I knew how to dress myself if I wanted to leave the house.

Yes, the irony of hiring someone to dress me so I looked like I could dress myself was not lost on me. But it gave me a comfort that nothing else could. Becca was good at finding outfits that were me—that I felt good and comfortable in—that I wouldn't feel embarrassed if I landed on the front page of a tabloid.

After sorting through the pages and matching clothes up with the pictures, I finally found something that didn't feel too overdone: a short skirt, heels that weren't going to kill me, and a rich, velvet-like red top. That seemed pretty safe.

Unwrapping my wet hair from the towel, I crossed into the bathroom and started layering in gook that would make it look less-than-flat for the evening.

"What time is your car coming?" I shouted to Connor where he was still lounging.

He could probably go out in track pants and a plain white t-shirt and end up on the cover of some magazine as a Hot In The City type thing.

"Mac's coming in about twenty minutes."

I flipped my hair over, running the hairdryer as quickly as I could, thinking "dry faster" so maybe I could get a bit of cuddle time before he left.

No idea why Connor was having Mac pick him up here instead of just waiting at his own place for him. It's not like I was getting ready to go out and rob a bank. It was just girls' night out.

I didn't know if it was cute or weird.

Probably both knowing him.

I slapped on some mascara and lip gloss and hobbled out to the living room, trying to get used to these shoes before leaving the house.

Connor was still in my chair, reading my latest *National Geographic*, which I'd magically started receiving on a regular basis. He looked adorable and sweet and comfortable.

I thought of the night ahead of me, the heat and crowds at the club. Wouldn't it be nice to just curl up on his lap and stay there for the evening instead?

I crossed the room to do just that, even though I knew the plan wasn't going to be put off and he'd have to leave in a few minutes.

Connor glanced up and his relaxed expression fell away and he stood, his gaze raking me from head to toe as I stutter-stepped to a halt.

"You're not wearing that out."

Note: That was not stated as a question.

"Yes. I am." Because, yes. And, I was already wearing it. And honestly, this whole getting dressed to be able to have my picture taken at any given moment because my boyfriend was successful at catching and throwing a little ball around was absurd.

He continued to glare at me. Well, my skirt. The glaring seemed to be mostly directed at my skirt. And maybe the shoes.

"It's kind of..." Connor glared some more, turning a bit to the side as if that were going to make the skirt not offend his delicate sensibilities.

I waited, wondering what he'd fill it in with... Short? Tacky? Out-of-style?

"Sexy." He said the word as if it were a curse, annoyed that he was having to spit it out.

"Sexy?" I was still trying to wrap my head around that idea.

Sexy wasn't a word people typically used to describe me. Even Connor. He'd tell me I looked cute or sweet or pretty. But never sexy.

My heart flipped over just a bit. A girl wants her man to think she's sexy once in a while at the very minimum.

"And this is..." I tried to come up with the right word to fill in the blank. I narrowed it down to annoying and bad. Both of which did not seem to match up with my emotional response to my boyfriend thinking I looked sexy. "Not good?"

Connor paced past me, giving me another sweeping head-to-toe glare from the rear.

"It's just the girls?" he asked.

"Going out tonight? Yes." Unless he was trying to ask if we

THE PROPOSING KIND   41

were going to an all girls club. Which honestly sounded like a pretty good idea. A place to have a drink and dance without dealing with Stranger Danger paranoia.

He shook his head. If there had been a chance of me knowing what the string of logic was he was working with, it was long gone when he'd asked that.

"Not even Dane?"

"Why would Dane be going?"

"Because you look like that and I'll be at a dinner smiling and telling people to donate money to a good cause where I can't do anything about the way he'll be looking at you looking like that."

I took a step back, almost tripping over the coffee table.

Connor was jealous? Because I was wearing a little skirt and leaving the house?

Granted, neither of those things happened on a regular basis, but it was just so... So *cute*.

Mr. Hottest Guy in Sports didn't want me leaving the house unchaperoned in a short skirt.

"What exactly do you think is going to happen with me looking like this?"

Because, honestly, I had no idea what he was thinking. Not that that was new. Following Connor's thought process was—obviously—becoming harder and harder to do.

"You're going to get hit on!" He ran his hand through his hair, glaring at the skirt again. "You're wearing heels."

He said that in the same tone that someone might say *you're stealing from your dying mother*.

I had *better* get hit on.

I mean, if I didn't get hit on looking like this, there was a problem.

"So?"

"So?"

I glanced at the clock, doing the math on how much time we had to humor his silliness before Mac showed up and saved me.

"You know what?" Connor pulled his phone out and started scrolling through it. "Why don't I take a cab to the dinner. Mac can drive you guys to...where is it you said you were going tonight?"

The tone that came out in was far, *far* too innocent compared to the outraged *So?* of a moment ago.

"I didn't say." And suddenly I was really glad I hadn't.

He glanced up, giving me a look I can only assume he learned from Abby. We stared at each other, just giving one another a bit of space in this ridiculousness.

"Hailey, where are you ladies going tonight?" He smiled, trying to smooth things over.

"I'm not sure. And," I smiled back, "I do not need Mac to chaperone me to make sure I behave."

Seriously, I had a boyfriend who had dated half the model population of the free world and he was worried that I was going to do something stupid while out with my girls. Was he kidding?

"What?" He took the last step toward me and wrapped me in his arms. "I completely trust you. You're the best person I know. It's *them* I don't trust."

I rested my head against his chest, feeling the rapid bam-bam-bam of his heart against my ear.

"I don't want to seem dense as this seems important to you, but who is *them?*"

"Them, Hailey!" His heart rate kicked back up. "Guys. The ones who are going to be hitting on you. All night."

"Aww." See? Cute. "Connor, just because a guy hits on me, doesn't mean I'm going to do anything stupid."

He huffed out a breath. "I know."

"So, it doesn't matter if a guy or two is friendly, because I'll just tell them I'm taken."

"A guy or two? Hailey, did you *look* in a mirror before you came out here?"

I pet his chest, easing him back down into the leather chair and curling up on his lap like I'd wanted to before he'd gotten stupid.

"I wish we could just stay in like this tonight." I barely mumbled it into his neck where my head rested. I felt him nod in response as his arms tightened around me.

His phone gave a little buzz from where it sat on the coffee table letting him know Mac was here. He ignored it, his head dropping back against the back of the chair.

"I'm going to go out tonight and dance and have fun with the girls. *I'm* not going to worry about the fact that *you* will be at an event surrounded by models all evening while you talk about the upcoming season and the potential something sportsy happening to sportsy people. Because honestly, why do men need models to do that? And then, I'm going to come home, take these shoes off, probably soak my feet so they don't fall off, and text you good night."

"That sounds nice," he answered, obviously only focusing on the last part of the evening. "Or, I could just come back here and see you when you get in."

Apparently that worry wasn't going away as easily as I'd thought it would.

"Okay. You could do that if you wanted to. But right now you're going to head downstairs because it's rude to keep Mac waiting."

"Right," he answered, but instead of getting up, he just tightened his arms around me.

After a moment, he rose, me still in his arms, and turned to set me back down, brushing a kiss across my lips first.

"Love you." Connor smiled, looking a bit more relaxed again, before grabbing his coat and stalking out the door.

I watched it close and wished again for a night snuggled up on the couch for just the two of us before going back into the bathroom to fix my makeup.

EIGHT

I pushed my way into The Brew having absolutely no idea what to expect from a night out celebrating Abby's twenty-first birthday.

For some reason, as cantankerous as Abby was, she didn't come across as the type of person to go out and get wasted just because she was celebrating being on this Earth for a certain number of years.

But, who knows. She also hadn't seemed like someone who would stealthily push her way into our circle.

It had taken me the entire walk there to realize that Abby, while being an odd-shaped puzzle piece, had somehow managed to become, in her own outsider's way, a member of our group.

I also realized I was okay with that.

It wasn't a surprise that I was the last one to get there since Jayne and I were the only ones who lived outside The Village.

And I'd had to deal with a temperamental baseball player.

I glanced around at the girls, figuring out if I was over or under-dressed for the evening. Even with Becca's guidance, I was always afraid I'd hit things just a little wrong.

Jayne was looking her high-end artsy self, Kasey had the polish you'd expect of a marketing guru in the making, and Jenna managed to pull off Girl Next Door Goes Slightly Wild in a Very Safe Way.

We were missing one very important person for this birthday party. Abby.

"Where's Abby?"

John pushed his way through the divider from the kitchen, setting a paper-filled clipboard down on the counter before glancing at all of us.

"She and Sarah are upstairs getting ready. They should be down any second."

Oh yeah, Sarah.

She wasn't around as much, but she'd been coming to the group's game night with John for a while now. Even getting into the competitive spirit of it and bragging about her boy band knowledge. Funny how our little group had grown so much in the past year.

A few moments later, the stairs in the back of The Brew echoed with the tap-tap-tap of dress shoes tripping down them, a light, happy, hopeful sound of women about to do something fun.

Abby looked like a slightly cranky pinup girl. Sarah, of course, pulled off the city chic of someone who worked in a museum. Both looked great and I was, once again, happy for the binder, no matter how pushy Becca was about shoes.

John gave everyone a look then glanced back at Abby and Sarah.

"Okay, ladies, here's the deal. You're only going to Gloss, right?" He nodded when we agreed, because why would we want to go to more than one club as it was. "No one is getting arrested tonight."

He gave us all a sweeping look, pausing ever so slightly on one of us.

"Seriously?" Kasey glared back at him. "You have a couple *small* run-ins with the law when you're in a bad place and no one lets you live it down."

"Right." John gave her such a dad look I almost laughed out loud. "If anyone does get arrested, you're to call Max. Not your mom or me or the pizza delivery place because you're drunk and hungry. Max. This has already been decided."

"By who?" Kasey asked, as if she didn't already know.

"By us." John didn't define us, but I had a feeling *us* was everyone in the masculine persuasion of our group.

Honestly, that seemed fine. I doubted anyone was going to get arrested tonight, but with Kasey's track record, it didn't hurt to have a plan.

Since no one else argued with him, I figured they were all thinking the same thing.

Kasey, on the other hand, was glowering and I feared a mutiny. Not a good thing since Kasey With Ideas always lead to Kasey in Trouble.

"Okay, killer." I tossed my arm over her shoulders and guided her toward the door. "No one's pointing fingers. I'm sure you can get through a night of low-level debauchery without causing any international incidents."

"See! Someone has faith in me." Kasey gave everyone else a look that said she was over it and let me push her out the door.

If *no international incidents* was the bar for someone having faith in her, we were probably in trouble.

At the door to Gloss, we got in line and I realized why I didn't go out that often. The reasons were numerable and deserve a list:

- My friends don't need to go out to have fun
- It's really cold in this line and these nylons do not protect your skin from the wind tunnel that is this city

- People smoke
- Smoking is yucky
- And there are people. Just in general. People. Everywhere.

I was counting all the ways I hated going out when Kasey elbowed me.

"Was that your name?"

"Tate!" The guy at the door was shouting. "Is there a Hailey Tate here?"

I glanced at the girls, wondering what I'd done wrong already to be pulled out of line.

I raised my hand, trying not to look like a third grader being called to the principal's office.

"I'm Hailey Tate."

The man glanced down the line at us and then waved me forward.

"How many are in your party, Miss Tate?"

"Um." I did quick math because, seriously, we were a party now? "Six."

He nodded, made a little mark on his clipboard and then pulled the intimidating velvety rope aside. "Have a good evening, ladies."

It took me a moment to realize he was letting us into the club. That we were jumping the line.

Kasey gave me a shove from behind and got me moving.

As we went by, the bouncer asked, "Who's the birthday girl?" in a voice that sounded both amused and cynical at the same time.

All of us pointed to Abby and the man reached behind him and pulled out an oversized tiara.

"If you think I'm putting that on my head so I look like some

Beacon of Bling, you're sadly mistaken." Abby gave him a look that would have had a lesser man running out of The Brew to buy cheap caffeine elsewhere.

He smiled. "Mr. Ryan said you'd say that. He said to tell you, if you wear it and he gets a picture texted to him of you girls, he'll donate a thousand dollars to Puppy Paws shelter."

Abby was obviously torn. I mean, who wouldn't want to help save puppies? After a moment, she snatched the tiara from the bouncer and shoved it on her head, looking like a ticked-off princess.

"You texted him back when he asked where we were going, didn't you?" I asked. When Abby nodded, I just shook my head. "That was your own darn fault then."

"Won't happen again." She reached for the tiara as if to take it off, then shook her head and left it were it sat.

He hustled us all into the foyer where a coat check waited for us to get rid of all our layers and Abby caught a glimpse of herself in one of the many, *many* mirrors these places seemed to have.

"I really am going to need a drink for this," she said before turning and striding into the darkened area of the club beyond.

I followed, amused at this side of Abby, but a little afraid of what a drunk Abby looked like.

Once we got inside, we magically confiscated a corner of the bar. The bartender noticed Abby's tiara right away and came right over.

"Bride or birthday girl?"

I sucked in a deep breath at the question, the word bride pulling me up short.

It had been four days and I still had no idea what was going on with Connor.

I was trying not to push him to tell me either because I didn't want him to get the feeling I was wedding-crazy when I was happy with us. Maybe he'd blacked out that he'd brought up marriage. Maybe he'd taken a ball to the head at batting practice. I wondered if he suffered from concussions. That was something I really should know. Maybe I should ask him for a full medical history so I could make sure to watch for any signs of trauma. That didn't seem out of line, right?

I also wondered who his emergency contact was. With Gavin traveling, I'd hate for them to do something like contact his agent, Dex. That man wouldn't care what was best for Connor as long as he could play baseball—and Dex got his cut—everything else would fall by the wayside.

I could just text him real quickly and make sure that he was covered. Maybe contact that person and see if there'd been any brain injuries I should know about.

"What are you doing?" Kasey eyed the phone suspiciously. As she should. "No boys tonight, remember?"

"I need to check who Connor has as his emergency contact."

"Right now?" Kasey was used to my craziness, a slightly calmer, less-likely-to-get-arrested, craziness than her own. Even to my own ears it sounded a little odd. "You need to text Connor right now, in the middle of Gloss, during Abby's twenty-first birthday party, to ask him who his emergency contact is in case something happens between now and when you get home at two a.m.?"

When she put it like that, it did sound even more than a little odd. I was pretty sure sharing my theory about engagement amnesia wasn't going to help my case.

"Dex can not be trusted." This was a true statement—even in the off-season. But I could tell it wasn't gaining me any sanity points with Kasey.

"Hailey, put the phone away before I take it away." Apparently Kasey had started channeling my mother circa 2004.

I slid the phone into my tiny little bag and hurried to join the group. I guess the mystery that was Connor would have to wait until later.

Of course, I would rejoin the conversation at the most interesting time. Who knows what Abby said to him before he reached this point? The bartender was pushing a drink across the bar to Abby even though her glass was still mostly full.

"Baby," he all but followed the drink over the wooden barricade, "I'm all the present you need tonight to unwrap."

Abby looked at him as if he'd offered her worms.

"Does that work?" she finally asked, obviously curious.

"Sometimes." He gave her the cockiest smile I'd ever seen. And that was saying a lot.

"Okay."

My gaze swung back to Abby. She just didn't seem like the hook-up-with-the-bartender type.

The guy started to pull a pen out of his hipster bartender vest, when Abby continued, "Can we please have a round of... um...something..." Her gaze swung my way. "What do you guys like? Do you drink those frou-frou Sex and the City type drinks?"

I glanced at the bartender, trying to subtly slide his pen back as he realized the "okay" was "Okay, thanks for telling me" not "Okay, let's get naked."

It was interesting to see the bartender look so disappointed. I glanced at Abby again, giving her a more thorough looking-over. With her dark hair in the little loopy curls and her slightly retro dress and heels, she really was pretty when she wasn't scowling. It was funny how comfortable we all felt with her hanging out with us. Hopefully she was feeling just as comfortable with us.

From the few things John had let slip, she hadn't had the easiest life. I wasn't sure what that all included, but when you're twenty-one and living above the café that's become your life with no family and friends to speak of... Well, I doubted the problems of someone as capable as her were all her fault.

It suddenly felt really important that she felt welcome with us tonight. Not just a pity birthday or a tagalong on her own night.

"We need to do welcome to your twenties shots!" That sounded even more enthusiastic than I meant it to.

I could tell I might have gone over the top a bit from the odd look Jayne gave me before she shrugged and said, "Why not."

Bartender Mark dropped the shot glasses down in front of us and dumped a bunch of amber liquid in them.

"First round's on me, birthday girl." He gave Abby a wink before swaggering down the bar, leaving her staring after him with a confused-yet-annoyed look on her face.

She didn't seem to know if she should take him seriously or not. Poor Abby, looking like she needed to decide if she should go with her standard attack or just...smile.

Abby reached for the shots and started handing them out, force of habit. Before she could down hers, I reached over and covered it with my hand.

She looked startled and unsure. The last thing someone should feel if they were out with friends. It dawned on me that she was one of us no matter how much of an outsider she felt or acted. At some point along the way we'd let her in.

I liked the idea of that. She added balance to our group. She and Jenna were opposite ends of the friend spectrum. They were the true equalizers that those of us running around in the middle of that sliding scale needed.

"Slow down, birthday girl." I gave her a smile I hoped wouldn't freak her suspicious nature out. "Ladies, to Abby! Who has somehow, through her sweet and gentle heart, taken over a place in our lives with advice that even Churchill couldn't argue with. Happy birthday, Abby."

"Happy birthday!"

Everyone glanced our way as we raised our shots, guys immediately zooming in on the fact that there were girls celebrating with alcohol. Because that always ended well.

A hot rush of pink rushed over Abby's cheeks as she lifted the drink and sniffed it.

"Yeah. Not how it's done, birthday girl." Jayne took her own shot and downed it in what could only be considered a professional shooter move.

As we watched, Abby followed suit, making a face but managing not to spit it out. "So, that was…burny."

"Here." Jenna slid hers toward Abby, and shrugged. "I'm not much of a drinker."

"Really?" Abby asked. I wasn't sure if she meant *Really, you're not much of a drinker* or *Really, drink another one?*

When Jenna shook her head, Abby downed the next one and rolled her eyes back.

"Maybe it's time for some dancing…you know, before you guys have to carry me home ten minutes after we got here." She collected all the shot glasses and slid them into the bin next to us, bussing her own birthday party.

"You know you're not working tonight, right?" Kasey asked, giving her the side look she'd perfected with Max.

Abby just gave her a sweet smile that broke my heart because we'd never seen it. Whether it was from the alcohol or the inclusion I couldn't tell, but I was really glad that whatever it was, tonight was the night it would come out.

Jayne rounded us all up and herded us onto the dance floor where the real party began.

I put aside my thoughts of engagements and emergency contacts and Connor going for spring training or losing his memory—or his mind—and just let the music sweep me away. A night out with my girls. No need to flirt or worry about how I looked or do anything else that felt so necessary when we went out single. Just make sure Abby had a great birthday and a good time.

NINE

"Connor!" I opened the door to my apartment, shouting even though the room was dark. "Connor!" A large, half-clothed body stumbled out of my bedroom, a pair of shorts hanging on his narrow hips.

"Connor." I smiled at him. "There you are!"

"Here I am." He looked down at me as I pushed my coat off my shoulders and tossed it toward the couch. Oddly, it didn't make it that far. Maybe my apartment got bigger while I was out. That would make sense, Connor seemed to make everything bigger. I thought about going to get it and hang it up, but then I'd have to bend down. Bending seemed so tricky. And far. Far, far away was my coat. But my shoes were down there too and I needed to get them off.

Bending was going to have to happen.

Darn that bending.

Maybe...

I reached my hand down and headed toward the floor, plopping my butt right down on the end of the carpet.

See?

Down.

No bending.

"Hails? Everything okay down there?"

"I did it without bending." He should be really impressed.

"The falling? I saw."

"This wasn't falling. It was plopping. I plopped. Right down. And now I'm down with no bending. And shoes."

"Did you guys take a cab home?" He glanced out the window, checking out the road.

"Nope. I walked." And wasn't that a feat to be impressed by?

"By yourself?"

"Just from the door."

"Who walked you to the door?" Connor was looking all Mr. Serious. Not a good look on him.

I collapse back on the carpet giggling because that was a lie. Every look was a good look on him.

"No one."

He crouched down next to me, looking not quite angry, but not a happy camper either. It felt like an interrogation time...but with him taking my shoes off too, so win-win.

"Hailey, how did you get home?"

"We took a cab."

"You said you walked."

"Just from the door. The cab wouldn't come inside. I asked because of the pictures in case there were paparazzi and how much I hate them. But he told me," I dropped my voice to make sure he knew how gruff and mean the guy sounded, "Listen, lady. You're on your own from the cab to the door. And so I walked home."

"You walked home from the cab."

I pointed at him because, "Exactly!"

"Okay. Sounds good." He bent down because apparently he

was doing bending tonight even if I was boycotting it. "Let's get these shoes off you and get you to bed."

He finished with my shoes and then lifted me up, carrying me to my bedroom where he'd been sleeping without me.

I wrapped my arms and legs around him, afraid he'd put me down and go somewhere else. I nuzzled into his neck, thinking *Oh. I could stay right here. Just right here.*

He ran his hand down my back, a comforting move that put me almost to sleep. Just right here.

"Hails, let me put you down."

"No, thank you." I made sure my arms and legs were all set staying where they were and just...stayed.

"Hailey." Connor said my name in a way that made me wonder if I was supposed to respond in some way.

"Connor." There ya go. Nice response, Hailey Ann.

He laughed, a low rumble against my ear then turned and plopped down on the bed. Just right. No bending.

I adjusted my legs to keep a hold of him and thought I'd sleep just like that. Nice and snuggly.

Connor shook his head and ran his hand up and down my back, lulling me to sleep.

"How did I not know you're a koala bear when you get drunk?"

"What?"

"You? A little koala bear when you're drunk, all wrapped up around me like this and not letting go. I had no idea."

Something in the back of my head started waking up, wondering at what he just said.

How is it he didn't know that? What else did he not know? What did I not know?

There were probably tons and tons of really important stuff like this that I didn't know about Connor. Between that and the emergency contact information this was a night of revelations.

Could we possibly not really know each other at all?

"Who is your emergency contact?" It seemed even more important now. It was make or break. I didn't know. How could I not know?

"What?"

"If you get hurt, who is listed on your insurance to contact?"

"Um...my dad." Connor pulled back to look at me as if I'd lost my mind.

Didn't he know how important this stuff was?

But, his dad. That made sense. Much safer than Dex. But his dad was really far away. What if he couldn't get here in time? Maybe Dex would be better. And me. I'd want to know if something happened to him. What if no one called me? What if people didn't know to call me?

"What about me? Would someone tell me if you're not okay? You have to make sure people know to call me. I don't want to find out you're dead on Facebook."

Connor was shifting again, trying to unlatch my legs and arms from around him, but I was even more set on the nuzzling. There was no way he was going to get up and go die and no one tell me.

I felt the tears on my cheeks, panicked tears.

"Hailey." He pulled at my arms again. "What's going on? You need to let go just a little bit so I can see you."

I slid my arms down and then latched them under his arms instead of around his neck so I could look up at him, still holding tight.

"First of all, I'm not going to die. And if I did, we're like one of the most famous couples on the East Coast. I'm pretty sure people would know to contact you. And, I'll call my dad tomorrow and make sure he has all your contact information in case he needs it." He ran his hand down my back, giving me a look full of worry. "I can even add you to the insurance notification if you want. But, what is going on here?"

"It's just like you not knowing I'm a koala."

He looked at me, a long patient look, as I rubbed the tears into his shoulder trying to pretend they weren't there.

"My emergency contact information is just like you being a koala?"

"Yes! Exactly!"

He nodded, smiling down at me. "Okay. I see exactly what you mean and we'll take care of all of it tomorrow."

"Oh." Something didn't seem right with that. I wasn't sure how we'd take care of everything tomorrow, but it seemed better to tackle these things in the daylight. "Okay."

"So, maybe we could just go to sleep now?"

"Okay." I let him pry my arms from around him as he shifted us to lie down and pulled the comforter up over us before I snuggled back in.

"Hails, I'm not going anywhere."

"I know." Or at least, I thought I did.

TEN

I woke up the next day with a gut-sick feeling that didn't have to do with the alcohol.

It was becoming apparent to me that Connor and I had a lot to learn about one another before anyone could start discussing maybe talking about maybe getting engaged.

The ways we didn't know each other could add up faster than snails on a rock—or something. (Don't judge me, I'm hungover). And I'd never see them coming.

I had to do something to prepare. Both of us. But especially me. To make sure I was ready and knew what I was getting into if Connor had been serious about this marriage thing. The emergency contact felt slightly less urgent, but still seemed important.

From under my pillow where I hid from the morning sunlight, I could hear Connor banging around in the kitchen, probably happily making himself more caffeine with that space-stealing coffeemaker than any one human truly needed.

Glancing toward the door and seeing the luggage sitting in the corner of the room reminded me we had a relationship that meant grabbing your time together while you could. Spring training was a few short months away, and with it was Connor's move south for over a month. Today he was jetting off to California to meet with a new athletic wear company who was courting him to be their spokesperson. They were small but passionate, and they wanted someone who had the shine to bring them a lot of attention.

Of course Connor was on their short list. The question was, could they make him feel so passionate about their brand he'd be willing to pass up the type of money Nike or Under Armour could pay?

I wandered out to the kitchen, eyes half-shut and trying to ignore the cotton taste of my mouth, to find him dressed and ready to go. It had to be later than I'd thought.

"Look who's up!" he all but shouted at me, the masochist.

I wandered over to my stool at the counter and climbed it like it was Everest. Which was valid since it probably took as much effort. Where the heck was a professional Sherpa guide when you needed one?

"So, good time last night?" Connor set a cup of tea down in front of me. "Dancing and all that?"

"Yup."

He reached overhead and pulled the sugar out before slamming the cabinet door shut.

"You guys get a little crazy?" He grinned.

"Nope."

"No? Really?" He opened the silverware drawer, rattled it around looking for just the perfect spoon—the torturer—then gave it a hard shove shut.

"Nope," I repeated.

He laughed like Satan, a loud booming laugh I'd always found endearing until today.

"Hails, it's clear why you don't go out very often."

I laid my head down on the counter, trying to drown out all

noises of another human being within a mile of me. A cool hand landed softly on the back of my neck rubbing little circles there, easing the tension away.

"The bartender fell in love at first sight with Abby and every time we turned around there were shots." I turned my head a bit so I could glance up at him. "Did you know there seems to be a point where you've lost track of shots and are just drunk?"

"Yeah. That's called getting drunk." Connor looked at me like I was nuts.

"I'm not really a get drunk girl. They're so little...litttttle, tiny shot glasses. How do they hold so much alcohol? It's like a magic clown car glass. And then..."

"You were. Well, thank goodness you walked home from the cab all right."

"Huh?"

He chuckled—a kinder, softer laugh—and moved away.

Apparently I was missing something.

I tried to remember what it might be when his phone started ringing as loud as a boat horn. Connor gave a muffled answer all the way from the living room six feet away and then shoved the phone in his pocket while he pulled his coat on.

"Hails, Mac is here to pick me up."

I whimpered a little knowing there was an answer I was supposed to give, but unsure what it was.

His hand landed on my back again, giving it a soft rub. "I'm off to California. I'll be back in three days. You know all this." He swung his bag over his shoulder. "Why don't you take a bath? I'll text you when I land and you're back to normal."

"I'm never going out with Abby again." This must be her fault.

"Okay. So, I'll talk to you tonight."

"Yes. Don't run away with a model while you're gone."

"Hailey." I heard the reprimand in his voice. I really was

trying to get past the model thing. But it still slipped out sometimes.

"Sorry. I love you."

He kissed me on the top of my head and whispered, "Love you too, you little koala bear."

Whatever that meant.

ELEVEN

A hot bath and seven gallons of Gatorade later, I recovered from my second hangover ever. No idea what that bartender was putting in those shots, but I couldn't understand how I could have been that drunk. Or that stupid. I stretched out in bed wondering how I was going to motivate myself to move.

Of course, with Connor gone for the weekend and the girls probably feeling the same way, there wasn't a lot I needed to do...except work.

But it was Saturday and even writers deserved a day off occasionally—if their sanity could handle it.

I was stretched out on my couch watching Gladiator and wondering if Connor had landed in LA yet when there was a gentle knock on the door.

I thought about ignoring it, but feared that soft noise would turn to a loud, insistent knock and might as well cut that off at the knees.

My building was pretty good about not letting people in, and Mrs. Lyman called the cops and reported "dangerous intruders" every time a solicitor got in to go door-to-door. It made for some interesting hallway moments.

I opened the door to find Ms. Jansen from upstairs on the other side, smiling sweetly.

"Hello, dear. Is your young man home?"

I laughed at the traditional view of calling Connor my young man, even while I kinda-sorta liked it. There was something very sweet about thinking of yourself as half of something so real.

"I'm afraid Connor isn't here right now." I refrained from mentioning he didn't actually live here. "He's gone to California for some business meetings. He'll be back in a few days."

I was really hoping she didn't want autographs for kids. He loved to do that and would be disappointed he wasn't able to help her out.

"Oh, that's too bad." She looked past me like she didn't know what to do since Connor was away.

"Would you like to come in?"

"Oh, no, dear. But thank you." She looked around again and seemed to come to some type of decision. "Would you give him this?"

She handed me a card in an envelope. It was sealed. Which honestly was disheartening. I'm not good with my curiosity being stymied like that.

"Of course." I gave her my best smile wondering if I could just get it out of her. "Is there anything else I can do?"

"Just tell him I appreciate all he's done and...well, that's it." She gave me the loveliest smile and headed toward the stairs.

She was so fragile looking that whenever I came across her in the hall, I always felt I should walk her to her apartment. At eighty-four she was still, as my mother would say, a hot ticket. But a fragile looking one who should be escorted to her apartment anywhere that involved stairs.

But Ms. Jansen was extremely independent. Apparently she

still hosted a poker night the first Wednesday of every month. She and the HOA tyrant, Marjory, had it out last summer about her and her senior partners-in-crime wild ways.

I totally wanted to be her when I grew up.

I was deep in the world of Joan Wilder when, far across my tiny apartment, my phone started to buzz since I'd turned the ringer to vibrate.

I dragged my body up off the couch and across the room to my office-slash-coat-closet in the dining room to where my phone was plugged in after a hard day of Candy Crush. The phone stopped buzzing and I considered turning around and heading back to Romancing the Stone, but figured while I was four feet closer to the kitchen, I should take advantage.

It was time for microwave popcorn and Diet Coke. Dinner of champions.

Sometimes it was great to be single. Sitting around, watching my choice of movies in a worn-out pair of PJs, eating whatever I wanted and not sharing.

Way better than going out to crowded clubs.

Of course, it would be nice if someone were here to rub my feet.

And cuddle with.

And try to out-quote our favorite scene.

But, really. A girl sometimes just needs a solo night in to enjoy herself.

Which I would be getting plenty of when spring training rolled around.

The sad part was, I loved being solo. I never had a problem being by myself. Most guys didn't last through an entire book writing/publication cycle. I was used to that. But, in just a few months, Connor had managed to fit himself and his crazy schedule inside my life and my crazy schedule.

And now here I was popping popcorn by myself and wondering why it was so quiet.

The popcorn was done and I was pouring a healthy amount of vanilla extract in my Diet Coke when my phone buzzed again. I glared at it across the room. The worst that happened if I went and checked was I'd have it for more Candy Crush now that it was recharged.

But when I picked it up my heart did a little flip flop as I saw Connor's smiling face looking up from the screen.

"Hello?"

"Hails." Connor sounded tired...and relieved.

"I thought you had meetings all evening." It was hard to hide how happy I was to hear his voice. The text when he'd arrived was great, but disappointing.

He hadn't been able to talk because they'd landed so late that he had to go straight into a meeting with Dex to prep.

"I'm hiding in the bathroom."

I would have thought he was kidding except for his hushed voice and the flush that echoed in the background.

"Why in the world are you doing that?"

"This meeting is going on forever. These guys drink like fish, and honestly, you're a cute drunk but I've maxed out on adults who can't hold their liquor for the year." He laughed at the end letting me know he was teasing.

"Yeah, yeah." Like I had a defense. "Oh, Ms. Jansen stopped by."

There was a long pause on the other end of the phone before he replied. "She did?"

Either my Spidey senses were tingling or that was suspicious.

Or I was still a wee bit hungover.

"Yup. She left you a card for helping her out with something."

"Oh. That was sweet." He sounded relieved again.

"Are you having an affair with Ms. Jansen?" Because strange women showing up at my door and a suspicious acting boyfriend typically leaned that way.

"What? Hails, really." He actually sounded put out. "Even my powers of attraction are only so strong."

"Um, right." Who knew I'd have to humor him even from across the country? "Anyway, it's here for you when you get back."

"Great. Thanks."

Pause.

Pause.

Pause.

Okay, that was enough with the freaking pausing. My curiosity was obviously stronger than my restraint.

"Connor..."

"Hailey..."

"Why did Ms. Jansen bring you a card?" This seemed like a really weird thing to have to pull out the Direct Approach for.

"I helped her out with her moving thing." He said this like it was common knowledge.

"With moving something?"

"No," he went on in that hushed voice. "With her moving thing. She's moving."

"Ms. Jansen is moving?" My stomach did a quick flip. "How did I not know this?"

More change? The things I didn't know about my own community were adding up way too quickly.

"I'm surprised she didn't mention it while she was there."

Yeah. Me too. What was going on? Maybe she hadn't let the Board know and didn't want to put me in a tough place with

Marjory. Which, granted, we were already going head-to-head on enough things this year.

"I have to go." Another toilet flushed behind him. "I just wanted to hear your voice and break up the monotony of men arguing over who had the better career when none of them played more than two years."

I could picture him, sitting at the table, his whiskey neat in hand, wanting to scream, "Me! I had the better career! That's why you're trying to hire me if you don't bore me to death first!" But instead pasting on his public smile and trying not to nod off while fighting to keep his ego in check.

"Okay. Have fun!" I put a particularly perky upbeat on that, knowing that only one of us got to go back to popcorn, Romancing the Stone, and Candy Crush.

Because, no matter how awesome I was as a girlfriend, I was just as super-powered solo.

I glanced around the apartment again, feeling like I'd found my stride. All this change was just one more little bump in the road of world domination...

TWELVE

Monday morning I was back on track and off to the gym.

It was surprising how easy it was to fall back in my solo routine even though I missed Connor. Still, part of me wondered if I was relieved to have all my space to myself again... well the space not taken up by his Xbox, Keurig, clothes, and collection of athletically minded shoes.

The gym was nice. I got in a yoga class before heading home, enjoying one of those rare mid-winter days that was warm enough, dry enough, and calm enough to be outside without four coats on. Even so, when I got to my building I was happy to have the new sheltered foyer to hunt down my keys and get the door open.

Fine. Score one for Marjory—darn it. Foyers kind of rocked.

I was rummaging through my gym bag when the inside door opened. Perfect timing.

I glanced up to thank whichever neighbor was coming out only to be facing a stranger. In a uniform. Smiling.

"Ms. Tate. Welcome home." A stranger who knew my name. Um...

"I'm Dan, the daytime doorman."

"The daytime doorman?"

"Yes, ma'am."

A doorman.

Or, a *daytime* one.

This had more Connor's obsession with safety and the HOA written all over it. I tried not to glare at the man politely holding the door.

"And so we have you during the weekdays?"

"Yes, ma'am. I'll be here during the weekdays. And Joe will be working the evenings. And we're still looking to hire for the overnights and weekends."

Overnights and weekends. There was going to be a man standing in our brand-new foyer twenty-four hours a day. Not to mention the man currently standing there wasn't what you expected in a nice, little doorman.

This one was hot. And young and fit. Honestly, he looked more like one of Connor's teammates than a doorman. A doorman was like Frank, the older man who made me sign into my agent's office building when I went to visit.

"So you're here to let people in?" Because that seemed like a huge waste of money—and not a big enough job for Marjory to push for.

Dan looked for a moment like he didn't want to explain his job, but then heaved a sigh as if he'd known this was coming.

"We're hired to do a little more than that."

"Okay. Like what?" Because I was really confused about the sighing and such.

"Well, we'll screen anyone stopping by. We'll also buzz you to see if you're available and want to allow them up. Mrs. Lyman will no longer have a reason to call the police a few times a week about stalkers when it's just door-to-door sales guys."

That was a plus, but not so much that we needed a door guy.

Or guys plural.

"What else?" I asked in what could only be my new jaded dating-a-celebrity voice.

"We'll sign for packages and deal with repair and deliver guys."

This was sounding way too good for the deep sigh he'd given me.

"And?"

"We'll help the older residents with getting their stuff upstairs."

Again...too good. "And."

He gave the sigh again, his gaze slipping away as he mumbled something about his start date being really conveniently timed.

"And, we'll take care of security."

"Security?" Because this was the first I was hearing about it.

"Yes. Apparently there'd been some complaints."

"Complaints from whom?" This was getting fishier by the moment and I was going to have to nip this in the bud...or further up the stem apparently.

"I couldn't say."

Mm-hmmm.

"Complaints about what?"

"I really couldn't say."

Right. He couldn't say.

"So, basically," I unzipped my jacket because my anger was working up some serious heat, "there have been undisclosed complaints about undisclosed issues by undisclosed people and so you're here to make it all better."

"That's roughly what I would assume."

Right. Like he didn't know.

I gave him the squinty eyes.

He didn't cave.

Darn trained security people.

I didn't know who I was going to get to first, Marjory or Connor—who I suspect had a hand in this if he knew about the foyer. If Marjory was pressuring him to upgrade the building by basically blackmailing him with these *undisclosed complaints*, she and I were going to have quite the throwdown.

"Right." Because what was I going to say? It wasn't Dan's fault my tiny little, quiet building on a moderately okay not horribly priced street just a few blocks from a halfway decent neighborhood I could absolutely never afford was suddenly getting upgrades that didn't make sense to the average person. "Thanks. It was nice to meet you."

"You too, ma'am."

"Yeah. Except for that. Please call me Hailey." Because I was way too young to be ma'amed. And would be until I was eighty.

"Yes, ma'am. I mean, Hailey, ma'am."

Oh geez.

I climbed the stairs, pulling out my phone as I went because this was obviously a call-worthy event.

Connor's phone went right to voicemail so he must still be in meetings.

Of course, since I was in paranoid, suspicious mode, maybe he was on the phone with someone else. Someone who now currently was working at the front door of my formerly quiet, non-descript building.

Maybe it was better I didn't get him right away. I really needed to think this all through.

What was I going to say? What the heck are you doing putting really nice, tastefully done, one-way glassed foyers into the architecture of the building, and stationing good looking doormen who will keep us safe and care for the elderly folks? Yeah, that sounded rational.

Of course, rational seemed to be flying out the window right now, so who was I to judge?

THIRTEEN

I was crashing Monday night when the phone rang. Because I typically ignored the phone when home alone, Connor had changed my ringtone for his number. Last time was I'm Too Sexy.

Apparently this trip was If You Think I'm Sexy.

Yes—I was seeing the theme.

I rolled over, reaching for the phone without bothering to turn the bedside light on.

"Hello, Ricco? I've been waiting for you to call all night."

There was a sputtering on the other end of the line before Connor's voice came over with the lamest Spanish accent I'd ever heard. "Si, my little señorita. I apologize for the delay."

"Oh, that was just...horrible." I laughed out loud, so happy to hear his voice, bad accent and all. "How are you?"

He paused, and I wondered what was going on on the other side of the country where he sat.

"Good." He drew the word out like there was something else, something not good he may have to share with me.

"But?"

"Nothing. Everything's good."

"Really?"

"Yup."

"Anything you wanted to tell me?"

Pause.

"Um..." I could practically hear him thinking.

"Maybe, something local?" I hinted.

"Local to me right now?"

He sounded hopeful and I could picture him running through his Google Alerts looking for something he'd done on the West Coast that had landed him on a gossip site. I'm betting at this point he'd be excited for anything he could use to divert away from the new security measures here.

"No. This coast."

You knew the man was desperate. He'd probably even gotten a call from Security Dan to give him a heads up.

After a moment, he caved. "So, yeah. I kind of hired a front door guy."

"You hired a security team, Connor." The exasperation was clearly coming out in my voice. "You can't just do that."

"I didn't *just* do it. Marjory was being a complete *pain* about the paparazzi and stuff."

"When?" I demanded.

"What?" He sounded surprised by the question.

"When did she harass you about the security?"

"Oh. It's been pretty ongoing. I swear she knows when I'm coming over. She always manages to be in the hall or stairway when I'm coming up. I think she makes her cat watch for me."

"Really? Her cat?"

"Yeah. Unless she has bugged Dex's phone and figured out what he knows about tracking me from that."

"Connor, seriously."

"I'm being serious," he huffed.

Frighteningly, he may have been.

"Why didn't you talk to me about this?"

"The harassing or the door guy?"

"Both!"

This was the stuff that was flipping me out. Like the emergency contact stuff. Stuff we didn't know. That he'd do something this drastic without telling me... Well, it made me really nervous.

"I guess I didn't tell you about the harassing thing because I didn't really notice it at first."

"You didn't notice it?" How was that even possible? If someone was demanding things of me like a *security team* I would darn well notice.

"Do you know how many people approach me on a daily basis about stupid stuff?"

Oh. Well. Yeah, there was that.

"Okay." Because I'd been witness to it way too often. "But what about the doorman?"

He sighed, a different kind of sighing. And I realized he was taking this seriously. Which made me happy and nervous.

"I guess, I thought if you knew, you'd try to talk me out of it. You'd say things like, *Well, what if we're not dating in a few months*, or something and then I'd panic." He paused, the kind of weighted silence where you knew something else was coming. "I guess I just didn't want to know if you weren't thinking long term like I was or not. I wanted to pretend that no matter what, this was it and I was just taking care of things to keep you safe."

"Oh."

I mean...*oooohhh*.

"And, even if you dump me or something, I'd still want you to be safe. That was the deal I made with Marjory. That I'd cover the door for an additional year after the end of our relationship."

"You're covering the door?"

"That is not the part I was hoping you'd comment on first."

"Well, I wasn't planning on dumping you." It hadn't even dawned on me that he might worry about that.

"Oh. Well." He cleared his throat. "Good."

We both fell silent, an occurrence that I'm not sure had ever happened before. Maybe this was the time to ask about the maybe-engaged thing. But if he was wondering if I was going to break up with him...maybe not.

Which just made this odder all around.

"I'll let you go back to sleep." He cleared his throat again. "I miss you."

I struggled between the wanting to hear his voice and the dozing off thing, but ended up just saying "you too" and slipping back into my nighttime coma.

FOURTEEN

C onnor barged into my tiny apartment and I wondered again why we weren't spending most of our time across town in his glass-and-exposed-brick-modern penthouse. It wasn't like all the reasons that existed before mattered anymore. The paparazzi had laid off for the most part and his doorman really didn't have any information to feed anyone since we were out in the public as a real couple now.

Well, you know, an actual real couple. As opposed to when we were out in the public as a fake real couple.

Hanging out at Connor's should have been an all clear.

"So, Hails."

Connor stuck his hands in his pockets and hovered over me where I sat staring at a basically blank screen. "I went for a run today and made a big decision. I'm hoping you think it's a good idea." He glanced away, looking a bit skittish. "It's a huge commitment but I think you'll be happy with it."

I turned in my chair, trying not to panic that he'd finally gotten his mind wrapped around us getting married.

Which, if he thought proposing to me while I worked and he

hovered nearby in sweaty workout clothes was going to fly, he was more than sadly mistaken.

I stood up and put on my best stall tactic face. "Are you sure you want to talk about this right now?"

"Yes." He started pacing again. Never a good Connor-sign. "I'm kind of excited now that I've thought it through."

Well, at least he was excited. But honestly, if he wasn't excited before maybe he shouldn't be so excited now.

I brushed by him, heading for the couch where at least we'd be on a more even basis for whatever this conversation led to.

I couldn't believe here I was, about to say yes—or no—to my boyfriend—who I *loved*—about getting married. Especially since I couldn't think of a less romantic setting. I sniffed in his direction trying to figure out if he smelled sweaty and everything. And, now, *was* I ready? I'd thought I was and then it became a non-issue and I stopped worrying about all the friend-adding drama. But, if this was the big moment, was I ready or were they right?

Stupid emergency meeting. I was never calling an a.m. meeting again.

"I think this is going to be great." He grinned, so pleased with himself. "For both of us," he rushed on.

Which, if he didn't think it was going to be great for both of us, then we were starting off even worse than I thought.

"You're going to get a lot of use out of this arrangement." Connor took my hand and nodded as if it were a done deal.

Use? We were going to have to have another talk about his ego and my career.

Right after I saw the ring.

And decided if I was saying yes.

"I've decided..." He took a deep breath and I thought again that this was the weirdest proposal ever.

Of course, for a relationship that began with blackmail based off of our agents and a bet gone wrong, I guess nothing seemed too out of bounds.

He took another breath and smiled at me. "I'm learning to set down roots. Be a grownup. I want to do things right. So, I'm asking—"

"Wait!"

I didn't know. I didn't know if I would say yes or no. How was that possible? I was four words away from a proposal from one of the country's most eligible bachelors and I didn't know if should say yes.

I wanted to. I'd never thought about *not* saying yes. But all I could hear was Jenna's voice running through my head with doubt...doubt...doubt.

I mean, I *loved* him. I knew I loved him. And I even liked him, which figuring with how things started, was a minor miracle.

But was Jenna right about marriage so soon?

This was completely Jenna's fault. Before I was just panicked about what my life would be like. How it would change. That things were moving fast.

Now I had to worry about if it was even *right* because besties wouldn't challenge a proposal unless they had some serious issue. Right? It would have to be like world-ending-issues.

What if I was just blinded by his charm and abs. Was that possible? I mean, they were lovely abs. And he *was* charming. Although, to be honest, the charm typically annoyed or amused me. And I loved him I really did. He was—

I realized he'd gone on with his proposal while I sat there panicking.

"...Nick to become my full-time personal assistant. If it works out, he'll take over more of the management stuff. And he can do all that stuff you're always wishing you could hire someone once every couple months to do. Book travel for events, help with ordering stuff..."

Connor's voice faded out and a low, droning buzz filled my ears, weaving through my brain and trying to shove my eyes out of the socket from behind.

"You're asking Nick to go full-time?"

"Yup." He looked so proud.

"With you?"

"Yes. He'll have to dump his other two clients. Especially since he'll need to work overtime when you need him. But this will allow me to really focus on the important stuff and stop worrying about details. Having Nick on call has been great, but I think I really need to get my ducks in a row."

Did he just say *ducks in a row*?

"Plus," he went on, "I think it will be good for him."

"So, Nick..." I was still having trouble wrapping my head around this.

"Hails, do you not like him? I thought you guys got along." Connor scooted closer to me and wrapped an arm around my shoulders. "Obviously, if you don't want him around that much, it wouldn't work. I'll make other arrangements."

"No. I like Nick." Plus, he and Connor had become something of friends lately.

Last week I came home—to my condo where neither of them actually lived—to find both of them on my couch playing video games on my TV. Okay, it was Connor's TV because he said no one should have to watch the action movies—or SportsCenter—on an old box set.

But still, it was kind of surreal.

"Nick's great." I pushed on, shoving the picture of a delicate, understated diamond to the back of my mind. "I guess I was just surprised you decided to make that offer. I mean, if you're doing it because of my occasional travel and stuff, it's really not that often."

"No. It's not just that." Connor leaned back next to me,

pulling me into him. "I've just been thinking that I need to start making some grown-up decisions. I'm looking at how I'm going to transition into the next section of my career. See if I can start doing those guest interview segments. I'm already trying to shift my sponsorships away from things like Harbor Island Beer. I want to make sure I'm not missing anything or worrying about stuff I don't need to. I want to just be able to focus on life when I'm living it."

I laid my head against his chest, wondering how Connor had managed to grow up in such a short time. Especially since it took him about thirty-years to reach that point.

"Okay. So, when are you going to see if Nick's interested?"

"Huh." Connor trailed the tips of his fingers up and down the length of my arm, teasing under the loose hem of my t-shirt's sleeve.

"Huh, what?"

"I forgot I have to ask him."

I rolled my eyes, glad he couldn't see me, and settled in. That seemed to be his MO lately.

FIFTEEN

"So, I thought we could do something a little different today." Connor stood in my "dining room" at the end of my office-slash-coat-closet looking really expectant. For what? Who knows.

I glanced at my manuscript that was skimming along at a fairly decent pace for something that was brand new and thought about telling him to go away...and maybe even considered changing the locks on the apartment.

But Security Dan would probably just break him back in, so what was the point?

Plus, he had been gone all last weekend. Doing something together was a good thing.

I made a note of what was going on and where I thought it was going, saved my manuscript, and stood up to stretch the kinks out.

"Sure. What did you want to do today?" Hopefully not something like ice skating in the Common. Romantic and sweet, yes. Cold, also yes.

"I thought you could help me. I'm going to go to that store where we got the chair to do some shopping."

"For what?"

"I need to do some redecorating." Connor glanced around, not meeting my eyes. "My place is too much of a bachelor pad."

I considered pointing out that he was a bachelor, but since that was part of the problem I was having right now understanding where said bachelorhood stood, I passed on that.

I couldn't help but wonder about this sudden need though since he was never at his place. Maybe his parents were coming to visit. He had a small problem with the fact that his mother wouldn't let him pay to put them up in hotels. He tried to explain that he could buy her a small hotel, but she just saw them as a waste of money.

"What exactly is it you plan on redecorating?" I had a rough time trying to picture his apartment since we weren't there very often.

Beyond that, my apartment had The Chair. And a TV...and his Keurig...and an Xbox. Connor had also recently stated that it was closer to Nick's place. As if this made sense to me.

"I thought I could start by making it a little..." Connor glanced around my apartment, probably looking for the right word. "Cozier."

Cozy. For the first couple weeks we dated I thought cozy translated to tiny. Apparently in Connor-speak, cozy translated to, well...cozy.

I just hadn't thought of Playboy Athlete as being someone who would appreciate cozy.

"So we're going to the furniture store to get cozy stuff?" Because I wasn't really sure what that meant.

I glanced around my apartment and realized I'd never decorated it. It was a conglomeration of things picked up here, given to me there, moved from home to dorm to here, and yard sale stuff.

I pictured Connor at yard sales. I literally laughed out loud and he scowled at me as if I was laughing at him. Which made me laugh harder.

"Have you ever gone yard saling?"

"Yard saling?" Connor glanced toward the window, then back at me. "Don't those happen in the summer?"

"Yes, but I was just wondering if you had been to a yard sale?"

"Why would I go to yard sale?"

"I don't know." That really didn't exactly explain my question so just kinda left it there.

"Okay." Connor crossed his arms and watched me shut my works stuff down. "Can we going to the furniture store?"

"Sure." I thought of my leave-the-house routine, and figured I could be ready in fifteen minutes. I had this down to a science. "Just let me change and we can take off."

Connor pulled out his phone and texted someone, checked something, then nodded. I wanted to ask him why he had to text someone in the middle of our conversation but he was acting weird enough already so I probably wouldn't understand whatever answer he came up with at this point.

"Great. Take your time." Connor settled into The Chair with another one of his sports magazines that had magically been delivered to my house for a couple weeks now. He looked way too comfortable.

Maybe redoing his apartment would mean his mail would start going there again.

A girl could only hope.

We took a cab out to the furniture store, Connor asking lots of decorating questions as we went. It had gotten to the point where even the cabbie was chiming in.

Once we arrived, we wandered into the lobby and everything stalled out. Connor glanced around as if he expected all the answers to be right there in the entryway.

After a moment he suddenly got a relieved look on his face, his shoulders dropping into a relaxed stance, as he glanced past me.

"Oh look! There's Nick." Connor brushed by me, hand outreached to shake Nick's hand.

Nick.

Just happened to be in the suburbs.

At the same furniture store that we were.

On a random Thursday.

"Hailey, hi." He smiled a bit nervous. At least one of them knew you didn't bring your assistant on a date. "So, you guys furniture shopping?"

I glanced between them, part of me not wanting to injure the bromanceness of the moment, but yeah...no.

"Okay. What's up?"

The guys glanced at one another, each obviously trying to have some type of silent conversation and failing miserably.

Finally, Nick grinned and stepped back. "I'm just the PA."

"Right." Connor nodded. "So you should take the hit."

"I'm not taking the hit for this." Nick shook his head and stepped back again. He was going to be outside soon if they kept this up.

"No one's taking a hit." I gave them what I thought was hopefully a reassuring smile. "I just want to know what's going on."

"I told you this was a horrible idea." Nick turned his attention on me and grinned his skater boy grin.

"I thought," Connor began, looking like he was suddenly rethinking whatever the thought had been, "if Nick came with us then we could just focus on the redecorating and Nick could deal with the details."

I watched him struggle with if this was a good idea or not. It's like he'd completely lost touch with what it was like to be a normal person.

Nick just stood there grinning at me.

"You really have zero idea how to be a normal guy, do you?"

He stood there looking completely sheepish. It was—sadly—a bit endearing.

"Fine." We were already here and figuring out how Connor's brain worked right now wasn't going to happen. "But when this is over you have to buy Nick lunch too."

"Bonus." Nick opened up his iPad and pointed toward the living room sets. "I thought we could start with the main room and move on from there."

And that's how date afternoon with my man turned into a guided tour of home furnishings with his assistant.

SIXTEEN

I got home completely exhausted from the day.

I felt bad admitting I was glad to be alone, but I was kicking into high-introvert mode by the end of the shopping spree. Luckily Connor asked Nick about his iPad and when he found out that it was his own—and old—Connor paid for my cab and dragged Nick to the mall to buy him one "for work."

I doubted I'd see them for hours since the mall also was the place where video games lived.

Collapsing back on the couch, I put my feet up wondering what the day had been about.

We didn't just shop for furniture. We looked at paint colors and style choices and window treatments. The only way he'd need all this was if he was gutting his entire condo and starting from scratch.

That seemed extreme even for Connor.

So, with my apartment to myself again, I did what any girl would do. Took a bowl, scooped out some chocolate ice cream, and started the next chapter of my new book.

Maybe not every girl wants to spend time writing a book—otherwise known as banging her head against the wall—but for me it was the perfect night. Or rather, the perfect night on my own.

I'd just started to get hungry when the phone rang. Glancing at the clock I couldn't believe that it was already 7 p.m. Where had the afternoon disappeared to?

"Hello?" I answered, a little surprised that Connor had changed the ring tone again already

It was now Mmmbop, because he said no one could frown to Mmmbop. There was a lot more noise than I'd expected wherever he was.

"Where are you?" I shouted to make up for the background noise.

"Nick and I are going to grab some food. And then crash at my place and play Madden NFL." He drew it out as if it were a question. But I was all in with this idea.

"No problem." That meant Thai delivery! And an action flick while reading.

Most of that was okay, but Connor always watched me more than the movie when I read and watched at the same time.

Non-book people. They just didn't get it.

"I just wanted to let you know I wouldn't be home tonight." He coughed a bit and then backtracked. "I mean, to your place."

So, that was interesting. But not surprising.

"And, you know, Nick's here," he finished.

As if I wasn't already getting used to Nick being around. But it would be nice to own my TV for the night instead of watching them shoot things.

Part of me needed more time for myself. My condo was so tiny that it felt cramped with just me in it. When you added a larger than life athlete to the mix—let alone his new bromance buddy—it felt like a closet.

I couldn't help but be counting down the days till Connor would be out of reach literally. With spring training hovering in the future, not to mention baseball being the most travel-extensive of the major sports, I knew we were on borrowed time.

But I also knew I needed me-time and Connor needed guy-time, so I pushed the guilt aside at feeling relieved for the silence.

"You guys have fun." I was already pulling out the Thai delivery menu. "I'll just get some writing in and sleep with the blanket actually on me instead of kicked off the bed by a certain heat-producing blanket hater."

"Blankets are meant to keep you warm when I'm not there." I heard what I could only assume was Nick snorting behind him. "Enjoy your blanket."

I almost said *Enjoy your bro-date* but then thought better of it at the last second.

Three hours later I was stuffed, had watched a great indie movie online, and finished making plot notes for the next day.

Yup.

Done with everything.

Just hanging out.

All alone.

Just me.

Okay. I was bored. Bored out of my mind. Usually this was about the time Connor called to tell me goodnight if he wasn't here.

I needed to reprogram myself for when that wasn't possible.

I picked up the phone and figured Jenna was a safe bet since her boyfriend, Ben, was still in London waiting for her to come to her senses and use the open-ended ticket he'd given her before he left.

She picked up on the first ring, hopefully a sign she was just sitting around waiting to talk to someone too.

"Hey, what's up?"

"Oh, not much. Just thought I'd call and see what you were up to."

There was silence on the other end of the line. Probably because neither of us were phone people and she was wondering if aliens had abducted me and left a clone in my place who didn't know this.

"I'm at The Brew." The phone got muffled as she shouted to someone *It's Hailey.*

I glanced at the clock wondering what she was doing there this late. Abby should have closed by now. Unless Emily was there and something horrible had happened. Like she'd reprogrammed the music to something overtly cheerful.

"Is everything okay?" I asked, trying not to panic.

"Yeah. Abby's just closing up so we can go."

Wait. Jenna was going out with Abby?

"Where are you guys going?" Because I wasn't invited. No one invited me.

"Just to a late movie." She named an over-the-top sappy thing where everyone probably died in the end of some obscure disease that had actually been extinct for decades.

"Oh."

"You're more than welcome to join us." I could hear the laughter in her voice. She knew I wasn't getting out of pajama pants to go watch that.

"No. That's okay. I'll just hang here." Far, far away from sappy mush.

Jenna laughed and I heard Abby in the background say something that had to be mocking.

"Well, have a good time." Because what else was I supposed to say. "Bring tissues."

"Already got them. They're hiding the contraband M&M's."

We hung up after making plans to work together the next day and I went back to my perfect night alone.

Maybe there was something worth watching on... I glanced at the TV and wondered why we'd never gotten that puppy.

SEVENTEEN

I was at The Brew working when the FaceTime calls started.

"Hails, which do you find a more relaxing shade of seafoam?" Connor held up two shirts.

"Why do you know what seafoam looks like and why do I need to feel relaxed when you're wearing this specific shirt?" Because I was going to have to call this what it was: Weird.

"What if it wasn't a shirt?"

"Does this have anything to do with all the redecorating going on at your place?" Because if it didn't, I was going to have to ask Becca if Connor's outfits were Becca-approved.

"You got me." My boyfriend, stealth decorator. "So, which one?"

I'm not sure why this was so important, but I figured if he didn't want to make the decisions himself, I'd just pick one.

"I like the softer one on the right."

"Great. That's what Nick said too."

I wasn't even going to ask why he'd called Nick first, but then Nick's face popped into the screen. "Right?" he asked. "The other one has too much blue in it."

"Yeah. Exactly." Or, whatever.

Connor pushed Nick out of the way, told me to have fun working, and signed off.

Because, that was pretty much par for the course right now in how odd things were.

"What was that all about?" Abby watched me toss my phone in my bag and gave it the side eye.

"I have no idea. Connor is on a redecorating kick, but he wants my opinion on everything."

"Not a surprise. You heard what he thought of that decorator he hired a few years ago. And—" She abruptly turned and headed back to the kitchen.

"Wait." I all but shouted to get her attention. "And what?"

"Nothing. How's your muffin?" she asked, a smile that could only be seen as a benevolent shining on me.

"It's perfect. You know that. Your muffins are always perfect."

"I used a little extra cinnamon to give it a bit of a boost."

"Yup. Cinnamon. Tastes great." I stood and followed her to the kitchen. "*And*, what?"

"Well, I was just thinking..." Abby looked like I'd put her on a torture device and was threatening her life and limb. "Maybe he's going to ask you to move into his place?"

It was a question, but I was still suspicious.

Abby and Connor were oddly tight. I have no idea why, but they'd taken to each other almost immediately.

"Did he tell you that?" That would confuse the marriage issue even more. I still couldn't figure out what was going on with him, but with all these changes, I was still trying to wait him out.

Not to mention, waiting myself out as I made sure I knew what I wanted.

I knew I wanted to marry Connor. He was it for me. Period. But now I needed to decide if I wanted to marry him *right now*.

"No. But—has everyone been acting weird lately?" she asked, a hushed tone as if she was afraid someone would hear us.

"Omgosh, yes. Seriously. Everyone's been super weird. And everything keeps *changing*."

"Everything." She glanced toward the kitchen door, her usual disdain not quite as apparent.

"Right? Every time I turn around, someone is changing something."

"Totally." Abby sat down across from me. "And it makes it all like, well, are you trying to get rid of me?"

"Or do you just want everything your way and didn't see the need to ask?"

"Yeah."

We both sat there, nodding to ourselves. It took me a second to really process what Abby had just said.

"No one wants to get rid of you." I was surprised how upset it made me. Abby was one of us. "For real. You're not going anywhere."

"Yeah. Whatever." She shrugged.

"No. Seriously. Even if you do decide to go away for college, this is home." She needed to know. *I* needed her to know. "You come back here. You're one of us."

Abby stared at me, a long, hard to read look I couldn't find words to identify. I struggled against the silence knowing she wasn't someone who put more trust in more words.

After a moment, she shrugged again, a tiny, barely-there smile touching her lips and said, "Okay."

"Right. Okay."

And that was going to have to be that.

I mean, what more could life throw at me this month? The change machine had to be coming to an end.

EIGHTEEN

Amazingly, I was adjusting to the changes quicker than expected.

I got home from the gym and was happy to have the foyer with the dark windows. Happier still to have Security Dan there to open the door for me so I didn't have to fumble around finding my keys.

It might be annoying the way Marjory manipulated Connor into paying for all these upgrades, but it was definitely nice to have them.

I got into the main building and noticed a bunch of toolboxes and buildery stuff lining the wall.

At this point I wasn't above asking because my suspicion level was pretty darn high.

"Dan?"

"Hailey, ma'am. How was your workout?"

"Butt kicking."

"I bet. Connor told me you're pretty hardcore in the boxing room."

A happy little flush rushed over me.

The first time Connor had shown up at my gym I'd been annoyed at him. And myself. But he saw my daily workout as middle ground for us. He called me athletic and I was so pleased I forgave him for pretty much everything ever.

"So, what's up with all the tools and stuff?" I asked it in the sweetest, nicest voice I could come up with. It wasn't Security Dan's fault that everyone else had gone insane.

"Those?" Talk about false innocence. "The guy who bought the condo from Mrs. Jansen is redoing it."

Oh. Well, that makes sense. Mrs. Jansen is lovely, but her condo definitely screamed 1965. She'd lived here since she was a newlywed, and apparently somewhere along the line the condo stopped matching the date outside the building.

I was surprised it sold so fast since the other condo on the top floor had sat empty for a month.

"They're trying to keep to midday hours for the loud stuff, but they're going to be here seven days a week. They'll be using the back stairs for most things so you won't have to deal with this very often."

I laughed at the idea that tools sitting out of the way was something I'd have to deal with. Security Dan was way too used to dealing with rich people.

And Marjory.

I shuddered thinking of how much worse Marjory would be with money.

"Thanks, Dan." I headed toward the stairs, happy to know that one change going on around me was normal. "Have a great afternoon."

Maybe it was time for something normal. Maybe a nice girls' night in.

Just me, my girls, margaritas, maybe a good movie.

It had been a while and change was great, but tradition was important.

I headed upstairs and typed up an email for Jenna, Kasey, and Jayne. Then I added Abby. Then I thought about it and added Sarah.

Sarah was a few years older and probably had her own group of girlfriends, but what the heck. If we're going with tradition and change, we might as well do it up right.

My phone dinged right away from Jenna with an *IN!* text.

Even if it was just the two of us, it would be a good time. Jenna was a tiny little party in a box. If by party you mean, PG-13 and funny.

Kasey was in, but Jayne had a gallery she was assisting with a show that night. Sarah had her own girls' night. And Abby finally emailed back with, "Is this a pity hang?"

Oh for the love of stars.

I picked up the phone and called The Brew.

"Hi! This is the Brew Ha Ha! How can I caffeinate you today?" So not Abby.

"Hey, Emily." I laughed to myself picturing Abby glaring at her across the counter. "Is Abby around?'

"Can I tell her who's calling?"

Wow, she was efficient.

"Sure. Tell her it's Hailey. And when she says she doesn't have time to talk to me, tell her I'll have Jenna walk over there and handle this if she doesn't make the time."

There was a long pause and then muffled mumbling.

When Emily started laughing, I knew my extra instructions had been needed.

"What?" Abby demanded as soon as the phone was passed off.

"Get the night off and get your rear to girls' night." I wasn't putting up with this from her. She needed to learn better.

"I don't want to be the extra girl." I could hear the doubt in her voice.

I guess I didn't really blame her. It was tough to be the new girl. But, it was time for her to acclimate. If we were bringing her into the fold, she had no choice.

"Jayne's the extra girl. Just ask her, she'll tell you."

"Pfft. Whatever." But, I could hear her stifling a laugh.

"Abby, suck it up. You're stuck with us. Get Thursday night off. John can watch your new protégé close. Sarah's out that night anyway. And twenty-four hours gives you plenty of time to sulk about having to leave the building."

"Fine, whatever. I'll bring a cake."

Oh, super bonus. I didn't even think of her incredible gift with baked goods when I invited her.

"Excellent. I'm texting you the address."

"Whatever," was all she said before she hung up.

Oh, Abby. Never change.

NINETEEN

That night Connor got home from what he called a brutal workout and collapsed in The Chair before pulling out an iPad from the magazine rack he'd stuck between The Chair and the wall. I occasionally kneeled on The Chair and leaned over the edge to glare at the rack.

But, now there was an iPad there?

"What's up with the iPad?" Because apparently the only way I was going to know what was going on in my own place these days was to ask.

"Oh, well, I was thinking you didn't seem to love all the magazines and Nick says he gets his digitally. So, I changed all my subscriptions." He gave me a little smile and went back to his iPad reading.

At first I felt a little bad. I hated those magazines. They were clutter in my already small space. And they had just started appearing like ants at a picnic.

But I never said that. I struggled with where the balance of Connor feeling welcome and Connor taking over was. A few pieces of paper stapled together every month felt a bit extreme to be the breaking point, but for some reason they felt that way to me.

And he'd figured that out on his own.

Mr. Oblivious.

And changed to an iPad.

Of course, it gave him an excuse to buy another gadget. And he and Nick probably bought matching covers or something.

I went over and climbed into his lap, pushing his new toy out of the way and resting my head on his chest.

"Thanks for that." I reached up to kiss his cheek.

He let the iPad fall to the side and wrapped his arms around me.

"Hails, I know I kind of take stuff over." He huffed a sigh. "I'm trying to learn to fit into your life instead of shoving you into mine. Especially since the places you *are* shoved in, we don't have a lot of options about. So, you need to tell me this stuff."

I glanced around the little room and realized the things that had been adding up so quickly over the last week felt like nothing now. Of course I wanted him to be comfortable here.

I couldn't help but wonder if we were just living together now, or if once he got his place redecorated we'd spend a little more time split between them and on our own.

As if he could read my mind, Connor continued on. "I've never had a spring training schedule that made me think about anything other than *Am I in my best shape going into this?* But this year, I feel like my biggest worry is how we're going to make this work? How is it going to work having my girlfriend a thousand miles away?"

I felt a deep sigh escape as I thought about that too.

I worried the girls were right, that everything was just so rushed because of Connor's world and the schedule it forced on him for seventy percent of the year. But, when we were together like this, the angst was gone. It wasn't even real.

It was just us and we fit.

"I'll be better about sharing my space." Because, that's all he was really asking, right? That he could share my space so he could be with me.

"Hails, I don't want to take over your world." He kissed the top of my head. "I just want to be in it."

And really, was there anything better than that?

TWENTY

I was a new woman. I was a woman who would accept and embrace change.

Yup.

I told Connor not to show up Thursday night because of girls' night. I went to the store and got snacks and margarita mix. I was planning to mostess my hostess duties like a super heroine.

With Abby bringing something tasty that meant we'd only be ordering takeout if people wanted dinner too—the perfect night. I even went to RedBox and grabbed something that didn't have explosions in case we wanted to veg in front of the TV.

When Jenna showed up, she glanced around the living room like there might be something new there.

"What?"

"Where's Connor?" she asked.

"Why would Connor be here for girls' night?"

"Ummm..." Jenna just gave me her weapon-smile and breezed by, putting her stuff in the fridge.

"What?" Because, that was not nothing.

"I just thought—"

"What?" Pulling teeth was not on my agenda for the evening, but it seemed it was on Jenna's.

"He's just always here." Even though she stated it as a fact, there was an underlying negative vibe to the statement.

I had no idea what her point was. She wasn't always here, so I didn't understand why him always being here would bother her.

"So?"

"I don't know." She shrugged, as if this conversation wasn't secretly a Big Deal that neither of us was admitting out loud. "It just feels like he's swept in and took over your life."

I turned from her and walked to the couch, plopping down on it, a little surprised we were going there. Jenna was typically Ms. Happily Ever After, but apparently not for me.

"What about Max and Kasey?" Because Max was all about Kasey. He was around all the time. And, since he was Jenna's boyfriend's best friend that meant he was around even more than Connor. It was like there was our group of friends...and then there was Connor. And he wasn't allowed in.

"Well, Kasey doesn't want to be in a relationship, so Max is fighting a battle just to get her to let him pay for dinner."

I was trying to figure out what the right response to that was when my updated intercom buzzed and I had to go answer it.

"Hi, Joe."

"Ma'am." We still weren't past the ma'am thing. "There's a young person here."

Joe, the evening security person, was not Dan. Dan managed to make everything feel easy and laid back even as he protected the building from...whatever they thought was going to happen to the building and occupants.

Joe, on the other hand, acted like we were the White House and every occupant was the president.

So of course I liked to mess with him.

"Does she look suspicious, Joe?"

"I have to say, ma'am, she actually does."

I muted the intercom while I giggled and Jenna came over to join me.

I turned the intercom back on. "Is she glaring at you like she could take you out with a paperclip?"

"That's exactly how she's looking at me."

"Looks a bit like a pinup girl? Big eyes, lush mouth?"

"Um..."

"Is she carrying a cake?"

"Oh, yes!" Joe seemed relieved to have a question he could answer that didn't involve sexually harassing a guest.

"That's just Abby. You only need to worry if she's smiling. Send her up."

Joe's voice came over the intercom, "Ms. Abby, you're cleared for entry."

"What the hell is this, the Pentagon? Do you know who killed Kennedy? Is there an Area 51?"

Jenna and I were laughing our butts off, incredibly glad Joe hadn't hung up yet.

"Ma'am, if I knew who killed Kennedy, I doubt you'd be cleared to have that information passed to you."

Go, Joe!

"Humph." I pictured her giving him her *You'll drink the coffee I made you* look. "Fine. But I'm watching you."

There was a beat of silence before Joe responded. "No, ma'am. That's my job."

"So you think."

Then we could hear the click of her heels walking away.

I opened the door and stuck my head out, waiting for her to come up the stairs. As she rounded the corner, she spotted me and gave me an eye roll.

"What's with the Men in Black routine downstairs?" She

shoved the cake at me as if I'd forced her to bring it instead of her offering.

"I blame Marjory," I answered, before clarifying. "The HOA president." When they both just looked at me, I went on. "She's using Connor and his celebrity status to force upgrades on the building in ways that are absurd."

"And he's letting her?" Jenna asked, shocked this was going on.

"He said he didn't notice at first because people complain all the time and ask him for stupid stuff and favors. Then it became something that sounds a lot like emotional blackmail because I live here."

"Oh." Jenna stood there, arms crossed in her little general type of stance studying me. "And he just did it?"

"I didn't know what was going on until after the doormen were already in place. Then I told him to let me handle Marjory from now on. Apparently she all but has his schedule memorized and knows to grab him in the hall when he gets here."

"That's—horrible." Jenna turned and huffed off, apparently Team Connor now.

I gave her A Look because she couldn't keep swinging like this.

"What?" she demanded. "It's not like I can think he's being pushy *and* that it's horrible someone's taking advantage of him."

"Wait," Abby had taken off her jacket and joined me on the couch. "What's he being pushy about now?"

"See?" Jenna waved her hand in Abby's direction.

"See what?" Abby asked, not liking being an example of something she didn't know about.

"You agree that Connor is pushy."

"Yeah. Sure he is. It's part of his personality." Abby looked at me like she wanted to say *Why is this news?*

"Exactly," Jenna stated, looking like she'd just been vindicated in all her arguments ever.

"Wait, are you saying that's a bad thing?" Abby squished up her nose, confused now.

"Of course, it is."

Abby looked like she thought this was the funniest thing ever. "Right. Sure it is," she snarked.

"You don't think so?" Jenna was definitely in challenge mode this evening.

I was just sitting on my couch, watching my friends argue about my boyfriend, and wondering where Kasey was.

"Well, no." Abby shrugged. "I'm snarky. Max is controlling. Kasey is a walking chaos. And you're a bit manipulative. But no one is getting pissy about any of those."

"Wait, what?" Jenna's cheeks were so pink I thought she was going to explode.

I was a bit in shock too. I wondered if somewhere in my tiny apartment I had a panic room I didn't know about.

"You heard me." Abby crossed her arms, obviously doubling down on her snark.

"I am *not* manipulative." Jenna was all but vibrating with anger now.

"Really?"

I jumped up from the couch. "Does anyone want something from the kitchen?"

"Sit down." Jenna pointed to where I'd hopped up from and I, afraid to tick her off further, dropped back in my seat.

I glanced between the two of them, knowing that no good could come of this face-off and wondering why it had to happen at my place.

"Explain yourself," Jenna demanded.

"Oh, did that need an explanation?" For someone who didn't

think she was part of our group, Abby was asserting herself pretty well.

"I am *not* manipulative," Jenna repeated and stood, hovering above the two of us, glaring at Abby.

Abby glanced my way.

"Don't bring me into this." I leaned back as far as I could into the couch, hoping it would swallow me and maybe I could take a nap inside its warm, comfy stuffing. "I just want to have a girls' night."

Abby looked at me as if I was a betraying betrayal person. She turned back to Jenna, taking a deep calming breath, and gave Jenna a look that was almost pitying. "You mostly use your powers for good. I mean, you seem to have people's best interests at heart. And you're not *really* pushy. Or mean. But things are definitely going to go your way. It's usually, you know, smile number three. But, when you're desperate, you ratchet that up to a level four or five smile."

Jenna looked annoyed enough that I suspected she knew exactly what Abby meant.

"I'm not...*manipulative.*" Jenna glanced at me as if I was going to help her out now. "Just because I typically know what the best plan of action is, and I *sweetly* make it happen, doesn't make me manipulative."

"Suuuurrrrre." Abby drew the word out so that there was absolutely no denying what she really meant.

"I—"

"You know what?" I broke in. "I'm going to stop this right here."

They both turned to me now, but my sanity was already in question by everyone. I was in stopping this before anymore deal breakers were thrown down.

"Ladies, let's deal with one crisis at a time. Now me." I waved at myself. "I was planning on a nice girls' night. Having a margarita or two. Eating this lovely cake. Maybe we'd watch a movie and then tell the guys we actually played strip poker."

"Oh, I kick ass at poker." Abby looked so smug I didn't doubt it.

Note to self, don't play poker with Abby.

There was a stare-off brewing again, but I'm not sure what winning would mean, so I stood up and clapped my hands.

"What are you, a kindergarten teacher?" Jenna asked, still sounding put out.

"If that's what I need to be. If we're going to argue, we're going to drink." I headed to the kitchen where I'd already pulled out the blender.

Margaritas always made everyone feel better.

All our phones beeped and Jenna checked out the note.

"Kasey's going to be late. Her client has *issues*." Jenna put quotes around it and I could only assume that was Kasey influenced. "So, she'll be here later if she can."

Great. The best chance at a peacekeeper and she was working late.

Abby and Jenna made uncomfortable small talk while I tried to figure out where to go from there.

We were going to have fun if it killed us, darn it!

After some more awkward attempts at conversation, Abby stood glancing toward the bedroom where I'd tossed her jacket.

"You know what?" she said, "I should probably get going."

"No. Absolutely not." I stood up and blocked her way, forcing her to sit back down. Pointing at Jenna, I'd had enough. "You. Fix this. You broke it, you fix it."

"I didn't break it." Jenna looked as mutinous as I'd ever seen her. "I'm apparently too much of a manipulator to break something like this."

"Jenna, you attacked Connor. I still don't know what your problem is, but you know that Abby and Connor are good friends. *And* Abby didn't say anything that isn't true. About all of us."

"She didn't say anything about you." Jenna's glare turned to Abby, who glanced at me and mouthed *Sorry*. "Don't apologize to her. Say something mean about her."

"These things aren't mean. And I said something about myself."

"Say something about *her*." Jenna was shouting now and stabbing a finger at me like I'd been the one to rile her up.

"Fine!" Abby shouted back. "Hailey needs to get her butt in gear and get some self-confidence before she lets doubt and *friends* ruin her future."

Someone gasped.

Then I realized it was me.

Jenna glanced my way, looking like I felt.

Abby dropped back down to the couch then let her head fall into her hands. She just sat there, not moving.

I was done. Done with this. We were not these girls.

"Are you happy?" I asked. "You broke her! Look at her. All the fight's gone out of her. I didn't even think that was possible. One night with us. *One night*. And you broke her."

I sat down next to Abby and rubbed her back, making soothing noises in a way I never thought I would before.

"I'm working on it," I said softly to her. "I know I'm not exactly reliable when it comes to myself, but I really am working on it."

"I know." She turned her head to the side and glanced up at me. "You don't take his crap and that's good for him too. But the only person who still worries if you deserve him sometimes is you."

"And Jenna apparently," I muttered.

The room fell too silent for any of us to be comfortable. I

wasn't sure what to say. It felt like the ball was in Jenna's court but she wasn't jumping in to fix anything.

After a moment, when I knew she wasn't going to break the silence, I finally stood and crossed to the kitchen, silently cutting up Abby's cake.

I stood there, looking down at my little tray and thinking that my life wasn't where I thought it would be right now.

Even as I considered the fact that Connor and I still had a lot to learn about each other, I thought about the important stuff and wondered if we knew enough of that. If each of us knew enough of the other to make a good, true decision about life forever.

I took the margarita ingredients out and started to make the drinks. If we were going to sit silently, I was at least going to have some frosty goodness to enjoy.

The loud buzz of the blender chopping the ice up cut the silence, getting me that much closer to my strawberry goodness.

I carried the tray into the living room and set it down.

"It's not that I don't think you're good enough for him," Jenna said, staring into her margarita glass like it was a crystal ball.

I worked to reply, not knowing what I was going to say, but Abby nudged me with her knee and shook her head.

"It's..." Jenna glanced up then, looking everywhere but at me for a while until her gaze finally found mine. "I'm afraid to say anything about Connor. I know that you guys are getting serious—"

I went to break in. If we were talking marriage we were more than getting serious. We were serious and talking about getting permanent.

"No. Wait." She raised her hand to stop me. "We're in this weird place where I don't know how things are going with you guys. I *like* Connor. I mean, it's hard not to like him. He's likeable and charming. But..."

She glanced at Abby as if she'd find help there, but Abby

wasn't going to do anything but have Connor's back in this conversation.

"If I say anything bad about Connor, and you guys do get married, it's going to be there forever. There's no coming back from that. But if I don't say the things that worry me, and you marry him and it's not the right move, then *that* will be horrible too."

Instead of making me feel better, Jenna opening up only made me more worried. I felt the tequila from my few sips of margarita going sour in my stomach.

"Okay." Abby nodded, more to herself than to us. As if she were about to do something insane. Which, Abby's version of insanity might be worrisome. "What if we have twenty minutes where we're totally in a safe zone? Jenna can say some of her fears and we can know that they're temporary and never bring them up again after today. Hailey can talk about her fears without ever having them thrown back in her face later. Like purging. When you purge stuff, it's gone. Like, gone-gone."

I looked at her, the girl we'd had just outside our circle of friends for so long and felt suddenly grateful.

I took a deep breath, knowing no matter how much we called this purging, it might still be there years later.

"Okay," I finally said, glancing Jenna's way to see what she'd think.

"Really gone-gone, never to be discussed again?" she asked.

"Yes." Abby gave a sharp nod, decisive, argument ending. "Even to Kasey and Jayne. Even to Connor. They aren't here. This is only for here."

"Okay." Jenna glanced at me and smiled, a half-hearted nervous thing I'd never seen on her face before.

Abby glanced between us, and continued, "There are some rules. You can't argue with the person. You have to let them finish. Then you can—*calmly*—give a response. The person can give one response back. Then we trade."

"That's very structured." I looked at Abby like she was a superhero.

"Structure makes things run smoothly." She glanced between us again. "Jenna, you're the most worried, so you go first."

Jenna obviously didn't like this, but I thought it was fair since she was the one who kept creating these bumps in our relationship super-highway.

"I'm worried that Connor is comfortable right now because he has everything he wants. That you're part of some Connor-is-great package deal that makes him happy and makes him look good to everyone else."

I wasn't sure what to say to that. I just kind of looked at her, trying to get the words to make sense.

I turned to Abby, wanting to clarify the rules. "Am I allowed to ask a clarifying question?"

Abby nodded. "I'll allow it."

"So, you think Connor is using me?" I mean, was that what it boiled down to? That she thought I was just a cog in his celebrity power wheel.

Jenna made her thinking face—swished up nose, gaze lifted off to her right—working through her answer.

"I'm not sure he's doing it purposefully. Like," she continued, speaking slowly as if every word had weight—which they did. "Maybe he's being subconsciously swayed to behaving in a certain manner. He's got the nice girl with the good reputation. He's settled down. He's behaving himself. And now he's gotten to stay on his team and he's getting more interviews and he's off being courted for sponsorships. So, I'm not *saying* he's using you-using you. Just that maybe he's..."

"Using me?" I tried not to laugh at Jenna even now in the safe zone dancing around what she really wanted to say.

"Yes...but not on purpose!" That seemed really important to her.

I thought it through. She seemed to be thinking a lot of things.

"So." I glanced Abby's way. "I'm not sure I have a comment to that yet. Can I return to it?"

Mediator Abby glanced at Jenna, who gave a little nod, before saying, "Allowed."

"I'm worried that..." I sorted through everything in my head right now, not sure how much of it I wanted to share even with the rules. "I'm worried you guys will never accept Connor because we had a rocky start."

Understatement.

Abby nodded and turned to Jenna. "How do you feel about that?"

"Well, they did have a really rocky start and he didn't seem to come around until he realized he didn't have a choice and being with her would clean up his image."

I tried to think of it from Jenna's point of view. She'd had to watch me fake-date Mr. America's Sexiest Athlete Playboy. She'd known his reputation—of course, everyone knew his reputation thanks to TMZ and *People* magazine—but still. People change. The fact that we had to work through our immediate dislike of one another and the forced proximity to really get to know each other, to really see the other for who they were, made us closer than other couples might be at this point.

Or ever.

Abby glanced my way. "Do you feel like that's true?"

"Not really." I hadn't realized how much my friends *didn't* see. All the little things, all the thoughtful stuff, the moments where it was just us. "He made a lot of effort to make me comfortable, to keep me safe from the craziness of his world."

I thought about how he was still doing that—even at the risk of my heavy annoyance—with the doors and the security.

"He's changed his life a lot to fit with mine. I don't think this is him changing behavior based on positive outcomes. I mean... sometimes I can't get *rid* of him. I just want to write and he's all *let's go watch a game. Let's see a movie. There's this sledding place in Nashoba.*"

"Wait. He took you sledding?" Abby looked annoyed to have been left out of that adventure.

"Sledding?" Jenna asked, as if to clarify.

"Yup. We drove out to Nashoba Valley and went sledding. Then we had dinner at a bed and breakfast and came back home." I thought about more examples of Connor doing stuff in a way that meant we got to be together without fans—or my friends. Just us.

While Jenna seemed to be shifting from doubtful to thoughtful, I was struggling with my own thoughts.

I mean, this is why you have girlfriends—to challenge you when you need it. What if she was right? What if she could see the situation more clearly?

I didn't think Connor was using me.

But she had a point about the positive reinforcement. Maybe some of it was that.

But—

"I don't think he's using her." Abby finally spoke up, stepping out of her mediator role. "I get what you're saying, but Hailey's right. There's stuff in every relationship we don't see. She's just done it backward."

"What does that mean?" I do a lot of things in the wrong order, but this was a bit too much even for me.

"Well, girlfriends usually gush about their new guy and hide the bad stuff. You've managed to do the opposite. You're the only one who has gotten to really see Connor."

Jenna nodded, like this was my fault, like I'd purposefully been hiding him. I wasn't sure what to say to this. A lot of things rushed through my head and I squished them down.

"Hailey." Abby pulled my attention back. "It looks like you have your next statement to make."

It was almost like she'd read my mind. But *she* had seen Connor. She knew him. He wasn't afraid of her.

I took a deep breath and dove right in. "You guys don't include Connor in anything. How are you supposed to get to know him if he's just this extra guy who is sometimes around?"

"What do you mean? He's always with you on Sundays at The Brew."

"You've never invited him to game night."

"Of course he's invited to game night! He never shows up." She was almost shouting by the end.

"You've never invited him," I repeated.

"He's never come."

This was starting to feel a little *Yes, I did—No, you didn't* for me.

In the background, my phone rang Connor's song of the week and I ignored it, knowing that was the *last* thing this night needed.

"Okay, kids. That's enough." Abby took a sip of her rapidly melting margarita while looking intriguingly thoughtful. "Jenna, have you ever said to him, Connor, we're having game night Wednesday. We'd love for you to join us."

"It's Hailey's job to invite him." She crossed her arms looking even more stubborn than usual.

"Why?" Abby asked.

"*Why?* Because he's *her* boyfriend."

"What did you say to Sarah when you invited her?" Abby. That sneaky, sneaky girl.

Jenna's cheeks got pink as she admitted it. "That we'd love for her and John to join us for game night."

"And have you explicitly said to Hailey that you'd love for Connor to join you?"

Jenna and I both knew the answer to that. There was no going back now that she'd started this and she knew it. I could see she didn't know if she wanted to be more angry, upset, or embarrassed.

We watched as Jenna pulled herself together then settled into her answer.

"No. I haven't." She gave me a sad little smile. "I'm sorry. I should have. And I suppose that the time he spends with Abby and you would be why Abby likes him?"

"It's easier to dislike someone you don't know." Abby gave her a soft smile, looking not her snarky self at all.

"Okay. I'll get to know him better. See what he's like now."

"So, Hailey. You gonna check that message? It might be Kasey." Abby knew it wasn't Kasey. She was just being a little snot.

"That's okay."

"I mean, I wouldn't want to keep you from anything important."

"Nope. Really."

"I just—"

"Oh, just listen to your message," Jenna interrupted. "No one's going to get mad."

I dialed into my phone and hit my passcode before it was ripped from my hand and suddenly speaker phone was engaged.

"Hails." There was a deep sigh before the message continued. "I hope you're having a good girls' night. I was just thinking…I'm really not looking forward to spring training. First time for that. Maybe we could escape for a long weekend. Just us. We won't even tell Dex we're going and I'll leave my cell at home—in case.

I'll ask Nick to find someplace no one will find us and take pictures or talk to us. Maybe like a villa or something. You can read and I can lounge and watch you read and it will be...just us. Just us." He took another deep breath. "I love you."

Jenna was staring at the phone, her mouth pursed in a tight little knot.

"That's..." She stopped.

Abby handed me back my phone, looking a little smug to have invaded my privacy.

Jenna cleared her throat. "That was very...sweet. He seems to really..."

"Love her?" Abby asked.

Jenna turned her gaze my way, her face looking clear of worry for the first time since she'd gotten here, one of her standard Jenna Smiles breaking out. "Yes. He seems to really love you."

We all just sat there, soaking in the idea that Connor Ryan really loved me.

I'd known that. He'd told me before. Him loving me had seemed to just be a fact. Not this overwhelming tidal wave of a realization that you read about. Once we figured out that we didn't want to be apart—that we didn't want that false relationship we'd started with—it was just the truth about our hearts.

They beat together.

TWENTY-ONE

I woke up hungover—not from anything I'd drank, but from the emotions of just going through the twenty-minute safe zone.

I did feel like Jenna and I were in a better place and it was great to see Abby feeling like she was one of the girls.

On top of that, after last night, I found myself needing some Connor-time. Some sane, no Nick, Connor-time.

Washing my stressed-out night off me, I dried my hair then texted him to see if he was done with his morning workout and wanted to do something fun. I had no idea what that something fun was, but maybe he'd have an idea.

When that stupid song played again, I couldn't stop the little smile from creeping on my face.

"Hey, Hails." Someone sounded up and at 'em this morning.

"What are you doing today?" It was Saturday. Even pro-athletes got days off during off-season. "Want to do something?"

"Oh." Connor sounded surprised I'd ask. As if we didn't spend our weekends together typically when neither of us was traveling. "Yeah. That sounds great."

"Don't overwhelm me with your enthusiasm." Because, really, this whole weekend was about people not overwhelming me with positive anything.

"No. It's not that. I just let the morning get away from me." There was a loud thud behind him then a noise like someone was mowing a lawn or using a really, *really* big blender.

Imagine the margaritas!

"Where are you?" I asked, instead of what flavor margarita he was having for breakfast.

"Me? Right now? Where am I?"

"Yes. You. Where are you right now?" I had the urge to glance at my phone to make sure I'd called the right person. I heard him muffle the phone and say something, and the noise stopped. "As opposed to where is Nick tomorrow."

"Oh. Ha ha." Did Connor just fake laugh at a non-joke? "I'm at home."

"Really?" Why was I suddenly suspicious of *everything?*

"Yup. At home." He took a deep breath then continued, "You want to do something today?"

At least he didn't make it sound like it was an imposition. That he was taking time out of his day. I'd just caught him off guard. Everyone lost track of time sometimes, right?

"I was thinking we could do something fun."

"Great! What would you like to do?" he asked, and I knew that no matter what I said, he'd be up for it. He'd do anything that would make me happy.

But, would it make him happy?

"What do you want to do?" I asked, trying to put the ball back in his court.

"Anything sounds good," he answered, sounding a little distracted before there was a loud thud like he'd dropped something heavy.

"Are you okay?" What was going on over there? Was he ripping walls down?

"Yup. Everything's fine. All good here. Nothing going on at all."

Okay. So everything was fine and we could do whatever I wanted to do.

This was *not right*. Not right at all.

I didn't want to do whatever I wanted to do.

Yes. I know how that sounded, but I wasn't insane.

What if we spent all this time with him letting us do what I wanted to do until he realized we never did anything he wanted to do and then suddenly we realized we had nothing in common and then life was a mess and we had to tell the dog we were getting a divorce and we'd fight over custody of him and I'd only get to have him here when Connor was on the road?

"Hails?"

"What? Sorry."

"I said, do you know what you want to do today?"

"Umm..." I panicked.

There was no other way to look at this. I was in a full-blown panic.

We couldn't get married. We shouldn't even date. We should just call this whole thing off right now. I mean, what would we be doing in a year from now. I had no idea how to hold this relationship together.

"Hails?" Connor was starting to sound worried. "What's going on?"

"I don't know what to do!" I meant about us, but when he chuckled I realized he thought I meant in general.

"Well, we'd talked about going to that space exhibit before it was gone. I saw the smaller version last summer with my mom in Chicago. I think you'd really like it and I'd like to see the other pieces that were traveling separately. Or we could go down to that bakery on the south shore we saw on the local diner show. It's Saturday, but we could get something to go. Did you want to go see the shelter I was donating Abby's birthday money too? I wanted to see what they were doing with it and you could play with the puppies."

As he listed things, I felt the stress drain right out of my body.

Why hadn't I thought of any of those? This was how it was supposed to be. Off the top of his head he listed a bunch of things we could do we'd both love.

"Oh." He jumped back in. "Gavin is having people over for something tonight if we wanted to go."

"For what?"

"I don't know. It's really last minute. He told some girl he met the other day he was having a get-together and I got an insanely panicked text from him last night begging us to show up."

Why was he just telling me now?

"Do you want to go?"

"Sure." I could almost hear him shrugging through the phone. "It's always funny to watch Gavin dig himself out of these messes. But I didn't want to say anything till I talked to you and...girls' night."

My heart melted.

I was an idiot.

"Yeah. Let's do Gavin's thing tonight." I liked Connor's brother and I loved that he accepted me so easily into their lives. They were besties. Which made me feel especially lucky to be invited into the circle.

"Okay. I'm off to write."

"Don't kill off anyone's favorite character."

"Ha!"

He hung up, and everything was right in the world again.

TWENTY-TWO

I was winding down, pulling myself out of my new world with its demons and mythology, when there was a knock on the door as it edged open.

Connor's head peeked around the corner when I glanced up.

"Are you at a good stopping place?" he asked.

I loved that. I loved him for it. He knew that he couldn't interrupt all the time. He knew that I had to finish thoughts and make notes and sometimes had to stay in the zone.

He said it was like a game where you were at your peak and you couldn't let anything interrupt your flow.

But I was at a good stopping point. Or rather, I had to be because my stomach had started growling about twenty minutes ago.

"Yup." I pushed back from my desk and stretched as he came all the way into the apartment.

He dropped a messenger bag inside the door that landed with a heavy thunk and I couldn't help but wonder if he was carrying rocks in that thing. Maybe it was a new pro-athlete workout. Carry heavy stuff everywhere.

"I brought lunch." He flashed me that smile that was literally worth a million dollars and headed toward the kitchen counter. "You typically get the tomato and mozzarella or the chicken pesto. I figured we could always just split them."

I grinned. Look at him all showing up here with my faves.

I went to kiss him on the cheek as I breezed into the kitchen to grab an iced tea and stopped.

He smelled different.

I panicked.

That was becoming standard operating procedure for me lately, but I'd just read in a magazine while standing in line at the grocer that if your man smelled different there was an 82% chance he was cheating.

But then I saw the accompanying sawdust in his hair and figured smelling like fresh cut wood wasn't the same as smelling like Chanel.

"So, you have a little something-something there." I pointed to his head, wondering what he was going to say about this.

"I do?" He brushed his head and watched, eyes wide as the sawdust drifted down like wood-man dandruff. "Huh."

I waited, wondering what would come after *Huh.*

Nothing apparently.

"Connor."

"Hailey."

Eye-roll extravaganza.

"Why do you have sawdust in your hair?"

"What do you mean?" Connor went to work opening the sandwiches...then stepped back and ran his fingers through his hair again to get rid of any leftover sawdust.

"I mean, *why do you have sawdust in your hair?*"

"Oh. Yeah. I walked through a construction site."

"So close you got sawdust?"

None of this was adding up.

"Okay. You got me." Connor turned and looked at me, and I suddenly was afraid of what was coming. "You can't tell anyone. Especially Marjory. But I had Dan sneak me into the top floor to see what they were doing."

"You and Security Dan snuck into the new condo?"

"Yup." He grinned and took a sip of his coffee looking way too proud of himself.

"Seriously, you guys are like five-year-olds. Next thing you know you're going to have Security Dan driving getaway for you and Nick at some gaming event."

"That." He pointed at me with a sharp stab of his finger. "Would be epic."

"Of course it would." I shook my head and set out plates and napkins before dropping into a seat. "So, speaking of construction, how's the redecorating going?"

Connor set down his drink and pointed at me again. "I am glad you asked."

Of course he was. I opened that door right up, didn't I?

Connor started a long explanation of all the different types of countertops a kitchen could have. I'd never known it was so complicated. But I also knew he already *had* a countertop.

"What's wrong with the countertop you have now?" Because, apparently I'd become the voice of reason in this insane shopping trip of redecoration.

"Nothing. But it's very...cold."

"Granite usually is."

"No, like it doesn't fit the homey atmosphere I'd rather have."

I half expected him to whip out Better Homes and Gardens at this point.

"Aren't those really expensive?"

"Well, they aren't cheap, but I'm not getting anything insane. Or tacky. It seems like tacky stuff is super expensive. Which, you'd think that would deter people." He looked at me as if I might have an opinion on this. When I just shrugged, he went on. "I asked the guy at the granite place and he said that there were people who literally just walked in and asked for the most expensive thing. He sold them this super ugly granite his nephew had ordered by mistake. He told him it was the most expensive thing he had and the guy bought it! Can you believe that?"

"Are you sure he wasn't making that up to get you to feel special?"

Connor gave me one of his *do you not know who I am yet* looks. He was oddly aware of people treating him differently and charmingly obvious to it as well.

"Also," he went on, ignoring my snark, "it's not like I'm getting enameled lava. That stuff is almost four hundred bucks a foot!" He seemed so outraged by this that I almost pointed out he was paid millions to play a game, but that conversation never ended well. And I'd already used my snark allowance.

"So, what did you get?"

"I'm glad you asked...again." He got up and grabbed the messenger bag he'd dropped by the door.

He proceeded to pull out granite samples and sort through them, explaining the special details of each one.

I never thought I'd say this, but I was beginning to miss my rough and tumble boyfriend who wouldn't know the difference between Luna Pearl and Rose Beta.

But, after an in-depth explanation of each of his samples, we moved on...to cabinets.

I couldn't help but wonder if the thrill was gone. If Connor's heated looks and hot kisses were a courting thing of the past.

If we'd secretly become an old, *old* couple without me noticing.

TWENTY-THREE

hen I couldn't get any details from Connor about what was going on at Gavin's tonight, I did exactly what Connor would have expected from every other girl he ever dated: I called his assistant.

Nick didn't know either.

But he promised to contact Gavin, find out what was going on, and if we should bring something.

I could get used to this assistant thing. It was way easier than trying to wrangle Connor.

An hour later Nick let me know it was a "nice but not formal" dinner party and that Gavin was having it catered.

And so, I found myself on a cold winter night, waiting for Connor and Mac to pick me up.

Luckily the Becca Binder had exactly the right outfit. The woman was insanely organized. I hadn't been a bit surprised when she'd shown up at my house in December with bags and bags of clothes and a letter from my agent, Catherine, explaining that a second season of wardrobe consultations (and clothes) was on her—a thank you gift for not destroying her after the Bet Heard Round the World.

I wasn't going to say no to having someone else do the shopping for me, but I was running out of closet space.

On the upside, the winter binder was up to date and had the perfect group date outfit. When Security Joe called up and said the car was here, I was ready to go, cute matching scarf and mittens and all.

In the lobby—or what was now a lobby—Joe glanced around outside as he held the door open for me.

I half wanted to shout, "Gun!" like in Miss Congeniality to see what would happen. But Joe was growing on me and I didn't want him to hurt himself throwing his body in front of mine.

Instead, I gave him a thanks and a smile and headed out to where Connor held the car door open for me.

"Hailey!" Mac turned around and gave a broad smile.

One of the reasons I didn't mind Connor hiring a car instead of taking a cab like a normal person was Mac. That and because then we didn't wait outside when it was cold—or he needed to politely escape his fans. Which, if we were being honest, his list probably went in the opposite order.

"Mac!" I grinned back. We were soul mates. I was convinced. "How are your grandkids? Good holidays?"

"I drove for the New Year, but the rest of the time they were here I got to spoil them rotten."

"Who'd you drive?" Connor leaned forward to join the conversation. The man was obsessed with celebrity gossip.

"Well, you know I can't say who, but it's an actress who was in town filming a movie for the week."

I could all but see Connor mentally running through a list of starlets.

"Any trouble?" I asked, knowing Connor was dying to know.

I just shook my head as he pulled out his phone and started Googling.

Mac drew the moment out, before giving me a little conspiratory wink. "Well, I'm really not supposed to say. You know I don't like to talk about clients—"

"Except that rock star who trashed your car," I put in.

"Yeah. Him." Mac shook his head. "But, this girl was…really lovely. I think you would have liked her a lot, Hailey."

"Oh." Connor flopped back. "Mac, you never give us dirt."

"He gave us the rock star."

"But nothing else. And we would have heard about the lawsuit eventually."

"Speak for yourself," I laughed. The celebrity world was one I was trying to stay far, far away from. "Plus, I like that Mac has ethics. I bet there are nights he's the only one in the car who does."

Mac laughed as Connor gave me a deep, unrelenting glare. "*I* have ethics."

"No one said you didn't." I patted his knee reassuringly.

From the front seat, Mac muffled his laughter.

We talked the rest of the way about the upcoming season and the new book I was working on. Mac was one of the few people I felt I could tell about it. Connor never asked because he knew I didn't like to talk about them while I wrote them.

The first night Mac had asked, Connor had checked later if he should suggest that Mac not bring it up, but there was something about the man that made you comfortable sharing anything with him.

He'd seen it all, as they say.

And so, Connor especially loved our rides because of the celebrity gossip and the inside look at my stories in progress. Probably in that order.

We pulled up to the condos Gavin lived in about midway

between Connor's high-rise and my little walk-up. His neighborhood was exactly what you would expect to live between the two places.

After Mac convinced Connor that, no, he did *not* want to come to dinner because the Bruins were playing, we headed into the building and left him to scream at his tablet over a cup of coffee in the underground lot.

Knowing Connor, there'd be a dessert plate sent down to Mac before we finished dinner.

Mac always thanked him.

Connor always acted like it was no big deal.

I always got a little melty with the reminder that my boyfriend loved to take care of the people in his life he truly valued.

As we got in the elevator and headed up to Gavin's, Connor reached over and took my hand.

"You know, I'm really glad you and Gavin get along."

I'd met Gavin months ago when Connor had come back from the first trip after our fake relationship had a very real breakup.

We'd both been worried.

Me, that he wouldn't like me or that he'd be some annoying hanger on.

Gavin, that he—also—wouldn't like me or that I was a gold digging hussy.

In the end, we'd hit it off. He was as kind as his brother but with a self-effacing humor that came along with living life just a *wee* bit overshadowed by a famous sibling.

The two were obviously close, or as my mom would say, peas and carrots.

And so, as we rode up the elevator, I was ecstatic we'd hit it off too and wanted to make sure that this woman wasn't after Gavin for any reason other than because he was pretty darn awesome.

I'd become one of those overprotective kind of sisters.

I was ready to break out the snark and vitriol to protect our boy.

Connor glanced down at me and grinned. "Why do you have your game face on?"

Oh! I had a game face! Sweet.

"Because I'm going to make sure she's good enough for Gavin or she's out of here."

He kissed me on the nose as the doors slid open. "There's my little fighter. Go get her, tiger."

Oh. I would. I was now a pro at this hot-famous-boyfriend thing. I would so go get her.

I mean, if she were mean.

Otherwise, I would be super nice!

Um, yeah.

TWENTY-FOUR

The door to Gavin's condo was propped open by a doorstop shaped like a baseball. Connor knocked on the door as he pushed it open and stepped back for me to pass.

Laughter floated out from the kitchen and I could feel Connor relax next to me.

He was even more protective of Gavin than I was. Even if he wouldn't admit it.

These two guys grew up as rough and tumble brothers. Gavin had moved here to "keep an eye" on Connor—read: enjoy hanging out with his brother.

But with that brother status came a lot of users and back-handed compliments.

But, Gavin was Gavin.

Here we were having an impromptu party because he met yet another woman who he was interested in.

At least this one didn't come via something to do with Connor. That gave me a lot of hope for the evening and I let my guard down as we stopped through the kitchen archway to join Gavin and his friends Pete and Andie at the butcher block island.

Pete and Connor did the whole hey-man-hand-slap-half-hug thing while Andie and I shook our heads. We were just getting to know each other, but bonded quite often over the ridiculousness of men.

Phrases like "hunting and gathering da'beers" was tossed out on a regular basis.

The caterer had dropped everything off just before we got there and Gavin was storing food in the pre-heated oven while the guys talked about the chance the Bruins would win that night —which was, as always in their opinion, high.

"So," Andie jumped in. "Tell us about this girl coming over. Where is she?"

"I told her to come at six thirty so I could make sure you were all here and on your best behavior first."

Connor leaned against the counter next to him and it struck me again how much alike they looked. It was amazing that a few shifts in bone structure changed Connor from just good looking like his brother to blindingly handsome.

I really should have ended up with Gavin.

I shook my head as I glanced between them again and Connor all but growled. "Stop it. That's off the table."

It was shocking that he could read my mind already.

I gave him a sassy grin. It was part of the rules of dating. I wasn't allowed to talk about dating Gavin again ever.

He wasn't allowed to go within twenty feet of a model.

These seemed like fair tradeoffs to us.

After some small chat where we all caught up post-holidays, there was a knock on the door and we all went still. It was like we were caught doing something we shouldn't have been doing. Andie broke the silence laughing nervously.

Voices traveled in to the kitchen as Gavin offered to take her coat and she said something in a low voice we couldn't make out.

As we waited, I realized I wasn't the only one waiting to pass judgment.

We were typically all fairly easygoing people, but Gavin's dating life was a sore spot for all of us. It was something the four of us had realized we were all on the same team over fairly quickly. Gavin had a gift for dating users.

And, while we were all ready to like this woman, we weren't expecting to.

Which was just sad.

After all, he'd met her at the coffee shop around the corner from his house. A nice neutral location for meeting another human being.

She came in, unwinding a silk scarf from around her neck and with a smile that said she loved everyone in the world.

I prepared to let my guard down as Gavin introduced her to Pete and Andie and then turned to us.

But then it was as if I was invisible.

"Oh, wow!" Irene flashed a suspiciously friendly-yet-surprised smile. "You're Connor Ryan."

Connor glanced from Irene to me to Gavin and I knew we were all wondering if the night was over.

Okay, all of us but Irene.

"It's so great to meet you." She offered her hand, something she hadn't done with either Pete or Andie. And, since she hadn't even noticed me, I doubted I was going to get the special treatment.

Connor being Connor, shook her hand and gave her as dim a smile as he could.

"Nice to meet you." He draped his arm around my shoulders and continued. "Gavin was just telling us how you guys met."

He was doing no such thing, but that's how the guys rolled.

We all shifted our attention back to Gavin who told us about seeing her at the coffee shop around the corner for a few weeks and having a nice conversation in line one day. Then the next week when he was at a table by himself and there were none left, she asked if she could join him. Instead of working, they struck up a conversation and he'd mentioned he was having people over tonight and invited her.

The wind wasn't completely out of his sails, but you could tell after Irene's reaction to Connor, things weren't going as swimmingly as he'd hoped.

Andie, being the ever aware friend, jumped in to redirect. "Would you like something to drink?"

"That white wine looks great."

We all made small talk while Irene glanced between us, her smile plastered on while she didn't add much to the conversation herself. After awhile, we shifted to the dining table, the guys carrying in food from the warmer.

Once we were all settled, I tried to bring Irene back into the conversation. I remembered what it was like to be the new girl here.

"Irene, did you know Gavin and Pete just got back from South America?"

"Oh," she turned to Gavin...finally. "Is that were you've been? I'd noticed you were gone for about a week."

Gavin grinned, obviously thrilled she'd noticed he wasn't around.

"We were in South America for about ten days. It was a great trip."

"Wow, South America." Irene looked suitably impressed and I felt myself relax.

Until she turned our way.

"Connor, you didn't go?"

"Nope. I'm legally not able to do things like that right now."

The pink tinged his cheeks. It always embarrassed him to admit he wasn't allowed to do stuff. Like a college kid home on break having a curfew. "Plus, Hails and I had some stuff going on that week."

She looked at him confused about why having plans with his girlfriend would have anything to do with anything.

"One of the reasons I had them over was to tell them about the trip." Gavin pulled the conversation back around to their trip.

Gavin told us how Pete was always late, so he'd make fake boarding passes for him so he'd be on time, but he'd forgotten to switch it out for the real one or the trip back. And chaos ensued! Gavin had us laughing so hard I had to put my wine down so I didn't snort it out my nose.

Irene just smiled along like it was a story she'd heard a million times.

"So, you guys must hang out a lot, right?" She looked about hopefully, her gaze landing on Connor. "Like go on vacation together all the time."

"Actually, we all have crazy work schedules." Gavin answered even though she continued to look Connor's way. I could tell he was trying not to lose patience. We had learned to be fair. People couldn't help but look at the famous person in the room.

It might mean nothing.

"But, when you're all home, you must go out a lot?" I could all but hear the *right? RIGHT???* On the end of her question.

"Not really," Connor lied through his teeth. "I mean, Hailey has her famous writer friends. And I have my famous athlete friends. So, there's not really a lot of cross over."

Andie looked at him like he was an idiot for saying such a stupid thing out loud, even as she knew why.

"Oh." Irene looked a little disappointed. Like her trip to Disneyland was really just to the local carnival.

The guys jumped back in to telling Connor all the great stuff he missed on the trip. Making the dangerous stuff sound even more exciting than it probably was so he really hated his contract.

Irene barely jumped in now. Just kind of nodded along to everything the guys said.

Pete had just finished telling a story about Gavin ending up on his butt while trying to set up a hang glider at the edge of a new cliff when Irene finally jumped into the conversation again.

"It really is amazing how much alike you guys look." She flashed at look from Gavin to Connor and gave Connor a smile I was all too familiar with from going out in public with him on a regular basis.

Next to me, he just wilted. I'm sure no one but me and Gavin noticed, but the energy just seeped right out of him. I slid my hand down to my lap then let it cross to rest on his thigh next to me. It took him all of a second to find it and wrap it in his own.

The look that passed between him and Gavin was heart-breaking.

Irene just kept going on, chatting about how Connor and Gavin must have so much in common and that it was crazy just how similar they were and how cute was it that Gavin moved here to be near his brother.

She was the only person unaware the date had already ended.

TWENTY-FIVE

Once Hurricane Irene had exited the condo, we all kind of sat in stunned silence around the table.

"So," Andie glanced around nodding as if we were all in agreement of something. "That happened."

I snorted, because, what else could I do.

"On the upside," Gavin stood and walked to the kitchen, "I waited until she had to head out to *remember* I bought dessert too."

Gavin—a man after my own heart.

We sat around, not being very kind to Irene and enjoying an amazing chocolate cheesecake. Connor finally felt like he could jump into the conversation and asked a ton of questions, making pointed guy slap downs at their stories and the pictures they pulled up on Gavin's tablet.

The rest of the night was great...but the weight of yet another woman using Gavin felt heavy to all of us.

I thought about hunting her down and using some of those power kicks Shawn had been teaching me. Or maybe Security

Dan could run a background on her. I bet he had connections at the local police. We could have her pulled over. If she had a car. Maybe she took the train.

I could have her mugged!

"Whatever you're thinking, stop," Connor whispered, shaking his head.

"What? I wasn't thinking anything."

"Right, like you weren't planning on having her kidnapped and extradited to a third world country."

"Oh." I kissed his cheek. "That's a good one."

Andie stood and backed away. "You two scare me and I have to work tomorrow, so we're out of here."

Andie and Pete said goodnight, Andie giving Gavin a long hug like that could fix the stupidity of his date. Pete giving the obligatory guy fist-bump and moving on.

I watched from where I loaded dishes into the dishwasher and Connor over-wrapped everything in plastic wrap.

When Gavin didn't come back to the kitchen, I found him in the living room sprawled out on his couch, staring at a blank place on his wall.

I tossed myself down next to him, putting my feet up on the coffee table next to his.

After a moment, he stuttered out, "I'm a little..."

"What?" I asked, honestly not knowing where this was going.

"I don't know." He shrugged, looking just like Connor when Connor was looking about five years old. "Jealous?"

"That Connor has a girlfriend?" I was more than a little surprised by this idea.

Connor had dated some of the most beautiful and famous women on the East Coast...and farther. The fact that Gavin would be jealous *now* seemed completely out of proportion with men and their altar worship at the feet of Sports Illustrated swimsuit models.

"No." He dragged the word out and I could see that he was already regretting bringing this up.

I pushed his beer toward him, wanting to give him a minute but still not wanting to let him off the hook on this one. I was Inquisitive Girl and I would not rest till all unanswered questions had been solved.

"I mean, Connor's dated some gorgeous women," I added, trying not to sound annoyed by it.

I must have failed miserably because Gavin gave me A Look. It made me wonder if he was picking up bad habits when he was at The Brew.

"It's not that he's dating or has a girlfriend or even that it's you. I mean, you *are* a goddess." He knocked his shoulder against mine and took a sip of beer. "But that's not it."

"So, am I supposed to guess what it is?" I was horrible at guessing. I'm that girl who congratulates people on their baby who aren't pregnant or guesses someone is *only* thirty-nine when she's thirty-one.

I should stay far, *far* away from guessing.

"I should make you guess. I need a good laugh tonight." Gavin gave me a should-be-patented Ryan Family Look. "But, I'll let you off the hook. It's not any of those it's more..."

I waited this time. It dawned on me he wasn't messing around. This wasn't just a passing statement. Chalk it up to my super-powered author observation skills.

Yeah. Right.

"So, Connor and I have always been tight."

"I know." They were more than tight. Sometimes it felt like they were practically the same person. Connor got—well, *anxious* wasn't the right word, but something when he and Gavin went too long without getting to hang out.

"But, that's changed since he started dating you." He rushed on when I went to jump in, feeling bad about being the Yoko Ono of the Ryan boys. "No! It's good. It's so good. He's more himself again. Even I like him more now. But that leaves me kind of on the outside instead of right next to him."

"Gavin, you'll never be on the outside." I thought about telling him the *Gavin's in South America* panic attack story, but figured if he hadn't mentioned getting married to Gavin, I wasn't stepping on that landmine.

"I will. And that's good. But, watching you guys tonight..." He shrugged again and I fought not to fill in the silence. "It was like watching people who had been together for years. You guys *know* each other. When one of you wants something the other already has it in hand. You laugh together at stuff no one else gets. Half the time you don't even talk, you just give each other looks. And there's that whole, this-reminds-me-of-that-time thing. I guess I was just used to being that way with my brother. But the best friend always gets shifted down a level when the soul mate shows up."

Soul mate.

It felt like everything clicked into place in that moment.

Of course, there were things we didn't know about each other. If we stayed interesting, active people, we'd always be sharing new stuff.

I was suddenly a ten-thousand-pound elephant lighter.

Reaching up, I gave Gavin a side hug and rested my head on his shoulder. "Thanks for that. But, you'll always be there with us. And when you find the right girl, she will be too. Nothing will break up the Ryan Boys Unit."

"See, that's why I love you." Gavin rested his head against the top of mine and we sat there just enjoying being in accord about one of the most complicated humans we'd ever know.

"Hey!" barked said complicated human from the doorway. "What is this?"

"I'm cuddling with your brother. Go away."

Connor looked between the two of us and shrugged. "Fine. I'm going to get another beer. Who wants one?"

And with that, all was right in the world.

TWENTY-SIX

We headed down to the car, hoping the Bruins game was over so we didn't disturb Mac. When we got there, he was reading something on his Kindle.

Connor waved him to stay in the car and opened the rear door for me.

"Mac," he said, sliding in next to me. "It was one hell of a night. Tell me the Bruins won."

"Two to one in the last forty-eight seconds."

"Nice."

If only I were a guy who lived and died by sports numbers.

"I take it the night was not quite as great as expected?" Mac backed out of the spot, heading us home.

I gave a play-by-play of Hurricane Irene while Connor glared out the window.

I know that it upset him more than he wanted to talk about. There was nothing greater he wanted than for his brother to be happy. And, if him being around got in the way of that, I wasn't sure what would happen.

Mac made the appropriate noises of annoyance. He was fond

of both Ryan boys and had probably seen his fair share of ladies using Gavin to sidle up to his famous brother.

It wasn't an easy thing to watch.

At my condo, Mac pulled over and wished me a good night. I took his paper dishes so I could toss out the end of his cake and hopped out of the car while Connor leaned forward and they had a quick conversation.

Those two enjoyed each other's company way too much. It was a trend I was seeing that I had to fix. To know Connor was to like him.

It was time my friends got to know Connor.

As we climbed the stairs, Connor slipped his hand in mine.

"I heard you and Gavin talking."

I figured he had. It was hard to miss in his smallish condo. But I wasn't going to bring it up if he wasn't.

"I'm really glad you guys get along so well." He squeezed my hand as we made the turn to the next floor.

"Me too." I wanted to add that he was like having a brother, but I was afraid Connor might read too much into that. Stuff I wasn't ready to say. Stuff I was afraid to bring up since he hadn't mentioned his fear that he needed to marry me again. "Gavin's too good for the girls he finds."

It made me wonder exactly how he was finding one bad catch after another. Of course, Irene found him so she didn't count. Then there was the girl *in* Connor's building. She'd narrowed in on Gavin as soon as she'd seen him. They really did look too much alike.

"Maybe we should dye his hair and get him some cool glasses." I pictured it in my head. "He'd look like Clark Kent. That would be pretty hot."

Connor stopped and gave me such an exasperated look that I couldn't help but snort.

"Really, Hails. My brother is off-limits."

"Right. But, we need to find him his Lois Lane. That's all I'm saying." I leaned into him. Just being there, being in the middle of my hallway with him trying to fix his brother's life—who probably wouldn't want us fixing it—was happiness for me.

"That's sweet." Connor wrapped an arm around my shoulders and pointed me back toward my door. "As long as Lois is some other writer."

"Yup! She's craftier than I am. She's also more willing to get into trouble. And she'll take on the bad guys. And she knows how to sway people to her ideas."

"So, basically, squeeze all you girls together."

I thought about it, and it was. We were, collectively, Lois Lane. How much did we rock?

When we got to my apartment, I pushed the door open and waited for Connor to follow me. When I turned around he was still hovering at the doorway.

"Mac's waiting downstairs for me."

"Oh." It had been a long time since he'd left me at the door. "Okay."

Connor all but laughed at me. "Please, Hails. You love your solo time. And I know you're kicking butt at your new project. And Nick and I are running a bunch of errands in the morning. So I'm going to head back to Gavin's, annoy him, finish cleaning up and have a beer, and crash at my place."

The tension I didn't realize I'd gotten when he said he was leaving all slid out. Of course he should go hang with Gavin. Especially since he'd been gone and come back to Irene as his welcome home.

"Alrighty!" I went up on my toes to give him a kiss good night. "Have fun with Gavin. Don't burn Irene in effigy or anything."

"I wouldn't do that..." He winked and kissed me on the forehead. "Not without you."

And with that, my man sauntered out the door.

I watched him go, annoyed he could get away with a saunter, then crashed, a book and a cup of tea my companions for the night.

TWENTY-SEVEN

The next morning, I rolled over and glanced out my window at the sound of plows.

Snow! Yes! Snow is like fairy dust. I hate the cold, but love snow.

Okay, maybe not all snow, but the first day of snow. I loved that. When it's clean and white and it paints over all the old yucky, dirty snow. It makes the dinge of the city in winter look like a winter wonderland instead of a freezing prison yard.

And so I knew what I had to do.

I had to go to The Brew for hot chocolate.

I layered up, then put on a fleece that fit under my wool pea coat. Add two scarves and some heavy-duty mittens and I was ready to go. I got to the lobby of the building and Security Dan leaned forward, a bit of a squint to his eyes.

"Hailey?"

"Yup! I'm off for hot chocolate." I glanced outside. No one was on the sidewalk. It was just going to be me. I loved how quiet it felt in town when the snow muffled noise and cowards stayed inside.

"Don't you have some upstairs?" Security Dan glanced toward the snowy white fluffs filling the view from the window.

"Yes, but not Abby hot chocolate." I pulled my hat down lower, tying the top of my fleece closed and double wrapping the scarf. I was off.

I crunched through the snow, only slightly annoyed at the corners that weren't cleared for pedestrians. Climbing over the stacks of snow and hopping over the icy slush of the gutter, I crossed my final intersection. The Brew was midway down a side block, the two gas lanterns on either side of the doorway a beacon in the white fluff of a wall.

I pushed the door open and breathed in the scent of coffee and baked goods, knowing this was the best plan I'd had in a while.

"Take your shoes off."

I glanced up at Abby, standing in the kitchen doorway, arms folded across her chest. "You're not coming in here with those clunky, mud and snow covered things."

I gave her a grin and acted like I was going to step off the doorway mat.

"Seriously. Don't even think about it."

"Abby, you can't refuse to let people come in if they won't take their shoes off."

"Yes. Yes, I can."

"No. You really can't." I shook my head at her. "I'm not even sure where you get the idea that you can. It's just weird. Even for you."

"I don't go tromping into your home covered in yuck."

"No. And I appreciate that." I pulled my mittens off and started undoing all my layers. "And I promise not to go upstairs and jump up and down on your bed in these, but you can't just refuse to let people in."

She glared. This seemed like a breaking point for her.

"I'm prepared." I reached in my bag and pulled out the Keds I'd brought with me. "But seriously, you can't just tell people they can't come in."

Abby gave a deep sigh—probably of relief—and returned to the kitchen.

"You're the only one who has come in. It's snowmaggedon out there," she shouted from the kitchen. "I thought I'd be safe to freeze dough all day."

"Then what is that scrumptious smell?" I asked, settling into my chair.

"Brownies. They'll keep overnight." She dropped into the chair across from me, glancing at the fire.

"Don't get comfortable. I want a brownie. And hot chocolate." I gave her a sticky sweet smile hoping we could get right to the chocolatey part of the visit.

"Fine. But, if you wait until you hear a ding, you can have hot brownies."

This was straight up bribery for her to sit and chill for a bit. But...hot brownies.

"I suppose I can wait."

Abby got up and went behind the counter. I heard the steamer making its magic noises and the smell of warm milk filled the café. She came back a few moments later, a mug in each hand, and settled back across from me, ignoring the computer on my lap.

"So, how was the party last night?" She took a sip of her milk goodness while I eyed the hot chocolate she'd set in front of me.

I caved to the power of girl talk and milky goodness. It wasn't like I hadn't gotten enough work done this week to start eyeing the beginning of actual writing time.

"It was great—except for the part where Gavin's date realized who his brother was and was all about us all going on vacation together."

Abby shook her head, clearly annoyed with the revolving door of users that Gavin seemed to have installed at the front of his apartment. "He can really pick 'em."

"She wasn't even good at covering." I felt the heat rushing up my neck again at the thought. "She even commented on how much they looked alike, as if that wasn't a dead giveaway."

Abby stared into the fire, sinking deeper into thought. "We've got to find him a woman."

I grinned, pleased to see that even Abby was feeling protective of Gavin. She'd probably adopted him vicariously through Connor. And, no matter what anyone said, I knew in my gut that Abby was one of the most caring, protective people I'd met. If you were one of her people, she'd go to the mat for you...probably while snarking you out for getting yourself in a position that needed defending, but still.

She'd be there for—

Wait a minute.

I glanced up again.

Gavin was a good guy who needed a good woman who would have his back.

Abby was a secretly sweet woman who needed someone she could care for in her rough and tumble way.

Maybe...

"No." Abby set her drink down and gave me a very serious look—way too serious for hot chocolate talk.

"What? I didn't say anything." I tried to look innocent as if I hadn't been planning to marry her off to my kind-of brother.

"You didn't need to. I know how you think." She picked her drink back up and took a sip, watching me over the rim of the mug. "I'm not marrying Gavin."

"No one said you had to *marry* him." Actually, I hadn't said anything.

Yet.

"Again, I know how you think." Abby took another sip that felt a lot like stalling.

"Okay, so I *might* have been thinking you and Gavin *might* be a nice match." It would be a great way to solidify both of them in our lives so neither could accidentally disappear or get left behind. And neither one of them cared that Connor was famous or rich. "But, if Gavin is a no, I won't mention it again."

"Gavin is a no." Abby stated this so definitively that I wanted to know why.

I sat there, all but biting my tongue to not ask. The Ryan boys were great and Abby fit into their lives probably better than I had in the beginning. I glanced at Abby again, suddenly wishing happy things for her—Bringing me back to Gavin.

I thought about my time with Gavin last night, getting a flash of ease when he said Connor and I were soul mates. A flash of rightness and acceptance. The deep knowledge that no matter what people on the outside saw or thought, Connor was it for me. And, no matter what the doubters thought, I was it for him. And that was something that was a big leap in acceptance for me. I was ready to believe that, no matter what, I was Connor's other half.

Then again...that was true for me, but maybe it wasn't true for him. I ran through the thought, pushing panic aside to consider that maybe I wasn't what he needed, that I wouldn't hold up to the life he led. That he would eventually not want me anymore.

That maybe he was my soul mate but I wasn't his.

I shook my head. Was that even possible? How stupid was I being?

Of course, I was his soul mate.

I mean, who else would put up with his ego? Who knew that he was secretly a bit of a nerd? That his family would always come first? That while he was cocky as anything he was also secretly unsure about people really loving him? Who got his sense of humor and loved that he was a celebrity gossip hound?

Me. Me, that's who!

I was Connor's soul mate!

I needed to marry him. Forget about him figuring things out. If he was going to be Mr. Indecisive, I'd just take the reins on this one.

I snapped my computer shut and set my drink down only to realize that Abby was sitting there watching me wade through the emotional awakening of my future.

"Whatcha doing?" she asked as I slid my computer into my bag.

"I have to go ask Connor to marry me." Because obviously, now that I'd made a decision, I had to act on it *right now*.

"Okay." Abby looked like this wasn't a big announcement. Like everything in my life hadn't just changed. Like I wasn't about to solidify my future with the man of my dreams. "But, maybe let's take a minute and think about this."

Or not.

"There's nothing to think about. I'm going to ask him to marry me. And he can say yes." Or no. But I wasn't going to plan for that outcome.

"Of course he's going to say yes." Abby smiled at me encouragingly. "I meant, let's just take a second and do this right. Don't just barge over there and say *Hey! Marry me!* I mean, at that level you might as well just text him *Wanna get hitched?*"

She had a point. This was a big moment. A once in a lifetime moment. I needed to do it right.

"I should maybe get him a ring or something." I sat back thinking about it. A ring didn't feel right. Connor wasn't much of a jewelry guy. But I felt like I should get him something permanent, something that symbolized the import of the moment and that he was promising to be mine.

I stood, pulling on my jacket as I did. Good thing I hadn't taken off all my layers yet. I'd just throw my boots back on and head off to buy some proposing supplies.

Besides figuring out the proposing gift, I needed to buy some champagne for when he (had better) says yes. And, maybe some of those chocolates from that French deli he liked because they ignored him like a normal person. Or maybe Abby could make us a little cake. What else did a proposing person need?

I'd have to set the scene. Something Mr. America's Sexiest Athlete would find romantic, and then I'd have to—

"Where do you think you're going?" Abby glanced toward the door where my boots sat.

"I'm off to buy a ring or something and proposing stuff!" I was almost jumping out of my skin. This was exciting stuff. How often did people propose to their famous boyfriends?

Okay, so I'd seen the pictures of women with *Mrs. Connor Ryan* t-shirts and *MARRY ME, CONNOR!* signs at the games. But this is for real. So, I was going with not that often.

"There's a blizzard out there." Abby sat back down, obviously expecting me to do the same thing.

"So? I got here, didn't I?" It was a great day to proposal shop. No one on the roads. I'd be able to get everything I wanted.

"You know not everyone lives above where they work, right? That almost everywhere out there is going to be closed. You just lucked out that you came here and my commute is a flight of stairs. Inside."

Closed. Oh.

Yeah, probably.

Foiled! By Mother Nature no less. Abby pulled out her phone as I fell back into my seat dejected.

I watched her slide through her phone, curious what she was doing, but still trying to plan my proposal so I'd be ready to go when the weather was done being a barrier to my personal bliss.

"Okay," she said. "I found a jewelry place on Newbury that Google says is open. Let me give them a call."

She hit call and waited until someone answered. "You're open?"

Someone murmured on the other end and Abby grinned, giving me a thumbs-up. "The green line isn't running, so we're going to be there in about forty-five minutes... Great. Thanks."

She hung up and shot me a grin.

"We?" I prompted, because I couldn't help but notice that Abby had included herself in my adventure.

"No one should do something this important by herself. I just need to grab my boots and as soon as the second batch of brownies is done we can go."

I was about to tell her she really didn't need to come when she smiled and all but shouted, "This is going to be so great!"

"Who are you and what have you done with Abby?" I leaned in, peering at her. "Emily, is that you in there?"

"Shut up." Abby headed toward the kitchen and I realized, nope. That wasn't secretly Emily.

I pulled on my boots as I waited for Abby wondering just what I was going to get at this jeweler. It wasn't something I'd ever considered. I'd barely thought about what *I* wanted for my own wedding ring, let alone what I'd do if I were the one proposing.

But Connor deserved something special. Something just between the two of us that he'd love. When Abby joined me, we locked up and headed out.

"The train app says the other line is running. Should we try it?" I pointed a mittened hand in the opposite direction. "It would only be two extra blocks if it isn't and minus four thousand blocks if it is."

"Not quite four thousand." Abby snorted, obviously no wanting to add to our haul.

"With the wind effect we might march in place for awhile and then it would feel like four thousand."

"All I know is you're paying for an Uber back since there weren't any available for the trip there."

You'd think I was forcing this on her.

We trekked down to the other track and lucked out when the train app turned out not to be lying. After a chilly ten-minute wait that felt like two hours, the train pulled to a stop in front of us. The driver did not look happy to see us, but we paid and headed toward the second car, figuring the glares would be less biting from there.

"I bet if they don't have rides for a certain time they get to go home." Abby leaned to the side so that she could see him glaring at us in the mirror.

"That can't be right. What if there's an emergency?"

Abby looked at me like I was nuts. I mean, what kind of emergency involved the T?

The writer in me immediately came up with two-bazillion.

When we got to the Copley stop we climbed out, ignoring more glares from the front of the train, and headed up the stairs. Dartmouth Street was no less cold than The Village—maybe colder because of the wind tunnel that Copley Square was. But there were more people milling around here. Even the drug store was open and apparently the place to be.

As we headed toward Newbury, I started getting warm. Then hot. Then absolutely sweating.

This wasn't that hard of a walk since most of the sidewalks had been cleared at least once since the snow started.

When I unbuttoned my jacket, Abby looked at me like I was nuts.

I couldn't believe how hot I was. Sweat started trickling out from under my hat. I stopped and sucked in a breath, trying to cool down and get my heart rate under control.

"What's wrong with you? You're not having a heart attack or something?" Abby took her mitten off and felt my head...which I'm not sure how that would have helped if I *were* having a heart attack.

I kept trying to slow my breathing, but it was coming in harsh, heavy kicks. It was making my chest hurt with icy cold air.

"Okay." Abby pulled me into a doorway. "Let's just take a minute here and not die."

"I'm okay." I was the healthiest of all of us if I did say so myself, so I refused to be the first to die. Unless it was some fluke like a crate of gold falling out of a charter plane making its escape to a small country that didn't extradite to the US.

We stood there—me breathing, Abby looking like she was going to call an ambulance. Or worse—Max.

"Let's just chill here," she said. "Or, that Starbucks around the corner on Newbury is always open. They might accidentally kill us with burnt coffee or mass produced baked goods, but they're open."

Leave it to Abby to be more upset about a café chain during my whatever-this-was than the fact that I was dying.

I was just thinking maybe I should take off my jacket when my phone rang.

Darth Vader's Imperial March theme.

Connor.

I pulled it out of my pocket and answered it, ignoring Abby's disbelieving stare.

"Hello?"

"Hails! Can you believe all this snow? It's great, right?" One thing I loved about Connor was that when it was just the two of us he could get excited about anything. He could be just a big kid.

"It is." I felt my entire body relax as he chatted on. I uh-huh'd and mh-hmm'd at all the right places until he started to wrap it up.

"I know you said you're writing this week. Just checking in before Nick and I head out."

How sweet was that?

Wait.

"Where are you and Nick going?" Because the two of them out in a snowstorm had the potential for disaster.

"Oh, you know. Just running some errands."

"Almost everything is closed," I pointed out, hoping to keep those two in. Or at the very least, making sure they called Mac to drive them instead of attempting it themselves.

"Right. We'll call ahead." Which meant he'd have Nick call ahead. But, whatever.

"Oh, have fun." There was one thing I'd learned—when Connor got something in his head, he was pretty much going to do it. And now that he had Nick as an assistant-slash-sidekick-slash-bromance buddy, I saw fewer and fewer moments of talking him down.

I hung up, feeling like somehow everything was right in the world again. My heart was slowing, I could breath—I was cold.

I tucked my phone away, ready to head back out. Another moment of clarity sweeping over me and brushing the panic away. Sure this was a big step, but it was the right one—the best one. My heart rate jumped again, but this time with anticipation, excitement pumping through me.

"Okay." I turned to Abby. "Let's do this."

TWENTY-EIGHT

W e got to the jewelers and weren't surprised to find it empty except for an older gentleman and a young woman sitting behind the counter, both of them reading.

When the bell over the door rang, they each looked up and the older gentleman gave us a kind smile.

"I was wondering if you'd really show up." He stood and walked down the glass counter to meet us near the door. "But it's letting up out there, so we figured we'd stay open since people will start to get cabin fever soon. I'm Jonathan."

"Hi, Jonathan, I'm Hailey and this smiling ball of cheer is Abby." I reached over the counter to shake his hand, feeling like this was already going well.

An empty store, a kind older gentleman, Abby to keep it real. Good plan.

"So, what can we help you with that you felt the need to come out in a snowstorm for?"

I glanced around, still unsure what I should buy but knowing after hearing Connor's voice a few moments ago that, no matter what, I was doing the right thing.

"I'm proposing and I need a proposing gift." It sounded less silly as he smiled and nodded. "I'm not sure what I want, but something that he'll like."

"Of course. I'm sure we can find something." Jonathan stepped down the counter toward the back of the room again leading us around the corner to where there was a collection of men's accessories and gifts. "We have a fairly wide collection of men's items. Some of the most typical gifts are, of course, a ring and a watch. Another option is cufflinks, but those can be tricky if your guy doesn't wear shirts that need cufflinks. There's always the option of an embossed leather band, something he can wear daily on his wrist. It's a bit more casual, but it wouldn't replace the specialness of a wedding ring when you say your vows."

That was a lot to think about. But he seemed ready to walk us through it, so I figured, until something struck me, I was just along for the proposal gift buying tour.

He motioned to the two cases with the corresponding pieces in them. I glanced over the rings.

I couldn't see Connor wearing an engagement ring. I figured when we got married he'd probably wear a thick, plain gold band, something I'd probably have to put a tracking device on so he didn't lose it when he took it off to play.

So, probably not a ring.

I glanced at Abby to get her take. She shook her head, echoing my no.

Plus, I'm not going to lie. I still kind of wanted him to get me a ring. Or to go get a ring with him.

I moved toward the watches.

This was a better bet, but I still wasn't sure.

"We have a wide selection of watches to choose from." Jonathan opened the back of the case with a little key and pulled out a few velvet-lined trays. "You can see that we can do a traditional gold watch with a gold band, or something in platinum. We also have some very nice timepieces with leather bands. Still as nice, just for a man who prefers leather."

I studied each group, not feeling anything click yet.

"We also have a small selection of pocket watches," he went on when I didn't jump at anything.

"Ohhh." He obviously had Abby's attention as she leaned to look at the pocket watches through the glass.

"Okay, can we see those?" I asked, figuring there was no harm.

The pocket watches were truly elegant. Several of each style were grabbing my attention, but I was feeling a little overwhelmed.

"Don't worry, Hailey." Jonathan smiled at me as he pulled the pocket watches out. "Most people don't come in and walk right to what they want. It's a big decision. I have men who come back six or seven times trying to pick out just the right thing. Don't feel any pressure to buy something today. You can work on your own emotional clock."

"You're very good at this," Abby said, almost scowling at him. Obviously seeing the opposite end of customer service was throwing her for a bit of a loop.

"This is what we do."

Abby nodded, probably figuring she was very good at what she did too and thus seeing no reason to change.

I picked up a pocket watch. There was something so elegant and quaint about it. I knew that Connor would really appreciate the beauty of it. He was something of a traditionalist in some ways. And it was something he could pull out for special occasions, not feel like he needed to wear it all the time because I gave it to him.

"How much do these things go for?" Abby asked, saving me

the embarrassment of sadly realizing that I was constrained by cost in a way my boyfriend wouldn't be.

"There's a range of cost. It depends on the maker, style, materials, and in some cases its rarity."

"So, are the used things more expensive?" Abby asked in a way that would have insulted most people.

Jonathan just laughed. "Sometimes. But not always. And used isn't typically how people think of them. Watches were, in a different time, built to last. Now, not all are. We've sadly become a disposable world. The workmanship on the newer watches is something you pay for instead of anticipate."

"Huh." Abby nodded, obviously finding this far more interesting than I would have expected her to.

A watch was a nice idea, but he did have several. All of them were tastefully expensive. Nothing too big or gawky...or tacky. I had a feeling that if he showed up with something like that, Gavin would have forced him to return it or mocked him mercilessly.

He didn't always wear a watch, probably because he was constantly having to take them off for practice, training, and I'm assuming games. So, that probably wasn't a great bet.

The pocket watches caught my attention again and I looked where Abby was oohing and ahhing over them. There was something intrinsically romantic about pocket watches. They call back to a time when time meant something. Time together meant something. Just like our time together—just like how it meant more because he was going to be on the road so much.

And, no matter how many times I got angry at Somewhere in Time about the lack of historical accuracy and completely ignoring the cyclical inability of the story's time travel component...a pocket watch still equaled romance.

Abby picked one up and clicked it open, smiling as she did so.

I couldn't help but picture it in Connor's large hand, watching him handle it with care like he did all things he valued.

I glanced down at the display again. They seemed to break down immediately into has-a-cover and does-not-have-a-cover. With how active Connor was, the choice seemed clear. I narrowed down to just the ones with covers. I also liked the idea of the cover popping open. It felt very old-timey, hot guy. I looked them over for something that felt like him—like *us*.

There was one with an intricate design of a thread wrapping into and over itself, filling the circle of the lid with four distinct corner points.

I picked it up, running my finger over the pattern. I loved the simplicity tying itself so complicated. It was like Connor himself, much simpler and also more complex than people ever imagined.

"Oh, that's a nice one." Jonathan pulled the light on the counter over, and set an empty velvet tray down between us. "It's silver, obviously. And the design is a Celtic knot known by many names, including a Celtic Shield Knot. It's often placed by someone for protection or to show the binding of two people."

Abby elbowed me when he said that in case I somehow missed it.

I clicked it open. The inside was beautifully worked as well. The face was a simple, clean white with crisp Roman numerals at each number under a clean, clear glass covering. The inside of the lid was smooth and obviously freshly polished.

"This is a nice choice." Jonathan smiled and I felt the truth of his words wash over me. "Too often people come in and want a Claddagh cover, not caring about the history or anything more than that everyone knows it. This has a beautiful background. We got this watch from an estate sale of a family who had moved here after losing their lands in Ireland. The watch, as the woman told us, was brought over by her great grandfather. It was one of the few things they hadn't sold for their move and had been handed down to the oldest son for decades. It was always carried by whichever child was traveling —for safety."

"Oh, that's lovely." I picked it back up and handled it, feeling the history of it.

"It keeps perfect time. Which is a miracle in some cases and just what's expected in others."

I fell more in love with the watch with every word, but I couldn't help to wonder why it was here. Where was its family?

"Why did they sell it?" I couldn't buy it, couldn't bring it into our newly forming family, if it was—tainted. That was the only word I could think of. If it were tainted from being dragged from its home, it wasn't for us.

Jonathan smiled, a bit sad but he also seemed pleased I'd asked.

"The woman who had the estate sale is the last of her line. She spent time searching down the last of another line, her grandfather's brother had gone to New York when he was a young man. We sent him an email for her because she thought he might like to have it. But—" Jonathan cut himself off and I could tell that what she found wasn't the heartwarming reunion a woman at the end of her life deserved. "She sold it to me with some other things. She's moving into an assisted living place that's lovely. The estate sale is going to keep her comfortable for the rest of her life."

I nodded, sad at the end of her line, but pleased that Jonathan had gone to the effort to help her.

"I don't suppose your young man is of the Irish lines?" he gave me a smile, knowing that here in Boston there was a good chance he was.

"With a name like Connor Ryan, I'm not sure what else he could be." I laughed, because, yes. Irish.

"Connor Ryan?" The question came from the far end of the

counter where the young woman had sat reading. "Holy cow, you're Hailey Tate, aren't you?"

Abby took a step forward, blocking my view of the young woman and all but raising the fur on the back of her neck... I mean, if Abby had had fur.

I leaned around her, knowing that now I *had* to be polite. "Yes. I'm Hailey Tate."

The girl rushed down the counter, her phone in hand. "You're Connor Ryan's girlfriend."

"Um, well, that's one way to look at it."

"Holly." Jonathan gave her a harsh look.

"You're proposing to Connor Ryan?" I could hear the extra question marks on the end of the question.

"Well..." Suddenly I felt very private. What had been a fun discussion with Jonathan felt intrusive with this Holly person.

She raised her phone, ready to snap a photo, when Jonathan's hand shot out snatching it from her. He turned back to me and Abby and gave us a tight smile. "Could you excuse us for a moment please?"

Before we could say anything, Jonathan had his hand wrapped around Holly's upper arm and was very firmly leading her to the backroom. The door fell shut behind them and Abby and I just stood there, a bit confounded for a moment.

"Maybe we should go." I glanced toward the door where the snow had slowed to just a light, pretty drifting. We could get some hot chocolate, mark this down as a bad call on my part.

"I don't think so." Abby was staring at the door to the backroom now, an intent look on her face. "First, we have to get your watch. Then I have to threaten that skinny, phone-wielding girl's ass."

Umm...

"Maybe not so much with the threatening." I mean, the thought was nice and all, but jail was bad. And if Abby and I ended up in jail we wouldn't be able to torment Kasey with her criminal past. "But I see your point about—"

"Connor Ryan!" came shouted through the back door. "She's going to propose to Connor Ryan!"

"You were saying about the threatening?" Abby quirked one of her perfectly shaped eyebrows at me as I was tempted to lay my head down on the glass counter in front of us and just give up.

After a few moments of muffled arguing, Jonathan came back out, Holly trailing behind him but looking mutinous.

"Hailey, I apologize for Holly's...behavior." Jonathan looked so embarrassed I was tempted to tell him not to worry about it.

Any other time, any other shopping spree, and I would have. But this was too important. Not only did I not want Connor to hear about this ahead of time and ruin the surprise, but I was pretty sure all paparazzi chaos would break out if this ended up on social media.

"We have a *strict* confidentiality agreement with all of our clients. Holly understands this." He emphasized this statement with a quick glare her way. "And, of course, the fact that you even visited the shop today will remain confidential. Isn't that right, Holly?"

We all turned to look at Holly who had returned to the stool she'd been sitting on. After a moment of contemplation, she finally flashed us a very big, very fake smile, and said, "Of course."

Abby all but growled next to me.

I turned back to Jonathan, not wanting to ruin the day with something as stupid as a Connor groupie and picked the watch back up, fingering the beautiful pattern on the front again.

"This is it." As soon as I said the words I knew everything was going to be okay. I was sure it was the right thing to do. I didn't want to have to wait to figure out what was going on in Connor's mind. I knew how he felt about me—not just because he'd told me, but because he showed me every day.

"Wonderful." Jonathan smiled, mostly absolute joy at someone who loved the watch purchasing it, and maybe a little bit of relief. "Do you want that engraved with something?"

That seemed like a good plan. But I couldn't imagine what to put on there not knowing when I was going to do the whole proposal thing.

"Perhaps you'd like to come back and have your wedding date added once you know it?" he prompted.

I could feel the relief rush through me. This is why you let the professionals get involved. I would have stood there trying to come up with something for hours. He probably would have ended up with a gorgeous pocket watch that said something stupid like "this keeps good time."

"That's a great idea." I fingered the watch one last time before letting him take it to package in a lovely little box.

This was about the time I noticed Abby had wandered down to the other end of the counter. The conversation going on down there did not look happy-friendly.

I tried to act casual as I meandered down to where the two women faced off, knowing that Abby could be tough, but I'd seen the nails Holly was sporting. It could get ugly either way.

"So, hey. Watcha guys talking about?" I asked, trying to avoid anything remotely like *How 'bout those Nighthawks* since that was pretty much exactly what I *didn't* want to talk about.

"Nothing," Abby replied, her gaze never leaving Holly's. "We're just having a friendly chat. Aren't we, Holly?"

Holly glared back, not backing down.

"Who are you? The Mafiosa?" I snagged Abby's arm to pull her back down the counter. "Leave the girl alone."

"Okay." Abby gave her one last smile. "I have Google Alerts and I know where you work. That's all I'm saying."

I gave her a small shove and headed back down the counter, not letting this get even *further* out of hand.

Jonathan handed me a delicate looking bag I was hoping would hold up to the weather, and an invoice I was hoping my heart could take. "Good luck, Hailey. I'm sure it's going to be a wonderful day and the start of an even better life."

It was such the perfect thing to say that I almost teared up.

As we were heading out I had a bit of a brain flash—and an idea to keep Abby from having to make anyone an offer they couldn't refuse.

"Holly." I stopped in front of the girl who was barely trying to conceal her annoyance with me for keeping my own proposal secret. "If I don't hear about my proposal anywhere before we announce it, when I come back to get the watch engraved you can Insta it with an announcement."

She narrowed her eyes as if she didn't believe me. "So, exclusive rights to the announcement?"

"No," Abby said before I had to.

"Well, no. Connor and I both have obligations because of contracts. But you'll have the first shot of the watch." You'd think the girl worked for *People* or something.

"Will Connor come with you?"

I said, "Probably not," as Abby growled.

"But," I went on, "this is better than nothing. Take it or leave it."

Jonathan made a coughing sound that sounded a lot like "confidentiality clause" and Abby did everything she could to look dangerous.

The idea that this girl was getting threatened from two angles and still thought she could pull something off was almost impressive.

"Fine." She crossed her arms, looking for all the world like she'd just bargained and won. "But you have to come in on a Tuesday or Thursday because those are the days I work."

"Holly." Jonathan looked like he was going to fire her anyway.

"Sure," I answered, wondering if she'd still be there.

I thanked Jonathan again and pushed Abby out into the fluffy white stuff.

The snow had slowed and the air was warm and dry so we walked along, peeking into the shops that were opening. Now that the cabin fever was setting in, or a dog needed to visit a tree, we had to share the sidewalks, but it was still peaceful compared to the typical midday traffic.

When we got to the turnoff where Abby would head back to The Brew and I'd trek on to my brownstone, she turned and gave me a smile so bright I almost fell back a step.

"I'm so excited." Before I knew what she was going to do, she threw her arms around me, then let go and rushed away.

I was choosing to take that as a good sign.

TWENTY-NINE

I wandered around my incredibly small apartment looking for a place Connor wouldn't accidentally stumble upon the pocket watch. I ended up putting it at the bottom of my tampons box. I figured it was safe there. But with my luck and knowing Connor, he'd decide tampons made a great replacement cork for a bottle of wine or something equally inane and go through the box this week.

Now that I had the watch, I was feeling ready to go—except for that whole proposing thing. I had to figure out how to do it... how to make him feel as comfortable and as sure of us as I did.

I was pacing around the living room-slash-dining area-office closet (twelve steps each way) and thinking it through. What would he feel was romantic? My first thought was that Il Giardino was the best way to go. Our first fake date had been there and I'd first noticed he wasn't the complete jackass he'd presented as during our first meeting.

Or our second.

But, I wondered if since we'd started the night basically

hating each other—and it was a *fake* date after all—if that was the best place to pop the question.

Also, it suddenly dawned on me he might say no. I wasn't sure I wanted to take that risk in public. I didn't think I wanted our proposal showing up online before we even got home—especially if he wasn't thrilled I'd become all independent woman of the new millennium and decided to go out on this limb.

He'd even talked one night about all the stadium proposals he'd seen and how they made him anxious because of all the things that could go wrong.

So, private was good. I was going to go the private route in case he—

The phone interrupted me, Darth Vader again.

"Hails," Connor started out without preamble. "Are there any types of lights that give you a headache?"

"What?" Was it me, or were his phone calls getting weirder? "Lights?"

"Yeah. Nick was just saying that some people get headaches from sitting under recessed lighting and I was wondering if you were one of them."

"Ask her about track lighting too," Nick's voice shouted in the background.

"I thought you guys were going out to play in the snow or something." Which sounded like the most absurd statement a girl could make to her thirty-one-year-old boyfriend and his trusty sidekick.

"We did, but snow is cold."

"So cold!" Nick added.

Okay. Valid.

"No. No headaches that I noticed." I collapsed on the couch, done with pacing for now. "Do you guys?"

"Nope. But Nick made a good point about them making

rooms feel bigger sometimes, so that's a thing." Connor hummed under his breath as I heard him flipping through papers.

"Yup," I said, because what else was there to say? "What are you guys doing today? Are you coming over?"

The phone was muffled and there was some urgent whispering I couldn't make out, then Connor came back to the phone. "Yeah, I'll be down—over—whatever— later today."

"Okay." Again, not sure what to say to any of that.

"Great! See you later. Love you!" Behind Connor's voice I heard Nick shout, "Like you!" and then the phone went dead.

I sat there with it, questioning my own sanity for wanting to marry into that.

A fter some heavy thinking, I decided to get a catered dinner from Il Giardino after all. That way, we'd have the romance of nostalgia but the privacy of my apartment. Mr. Antonelli offered to clear the entire restaurant for that night when I'd explained. That seemed more than a little bit insane. Also, I told him I couldn't afford that, but he seemed to see Connor as part of the family and offered anyway.

Once I convinced him I loved my propose-at-home plan, Mr. Antonelli had told me not to worry about the meal. That he'd send someone over with everything we needed by 6 p.m. and all I had to do was have a table to put it on.

And so, with a gift, a meal, and a plan in place, I called Connor.

"Hello?" he shouted into the phone over what sounded like a plane landing behind him.

"Connor?" Maybe someone had stolen his phone and was at the airport making their getaway.

"Yeah! Hold on!" The plane sound was muffled for a moment and then quieted. "Sorry about that, Hails. What's up?"

I tried not to ask him the same thing since he was the one acting weird lately, but I figured, asking him about the weird would probably just bring on another round of weird acting'ness.

"I was just calling to say hey and see what you were up to." Look at me being all nonchalant.

"Oh, you know. Hanging with Nick."

Hanging with Nick? This seemed to be his number one activity lately. Which, why was it no longer *Hanging with Hails?*

"Where are you guys?" I asked, because the plane and Nick and the weirdness all seemed to add up to the idea that the two of them together could not be trusted.

"Oh, you know. Just hanging out." He stopped talking and I wanted to just wait him out.

I bit back the, "No, I don't know. That's why I asked."

It suddenly dawned on me he was being cagey about something. Something that I was not in on. Something...with Nick. Okay, that was all I had at the moment. Obviously this would be my next mission after Operation Proposal. And now that I found that Abby was an excellent adventure sidekick, I'd suck her in on the mission as well.

But that was Future Hailey, and Future Hailey was happily engaged to the man of her dreams and doing silly things like dressing up in all black with her partner in crime, Future Abby, and pretending to be cat burglars to solve the case.

"I was wondering if you wanted to come over for dinner tonight?" As soon as I asked the question, my heart kicked up to an insane pace, rushing around inside my chest and bouncing off every rib and internal organ like some out of control pinball.

"Tonight?" He sounded like he was actually thinking about it. "Sure. Actually, tonight would be perfect. I can totally do tonight."

Okay. So, sudden excitement after odd, drawn-out thought process. That was good. That meant this weird behavior wasn't a way to avoid me after the maybe-proposal and then the never-mentioning-it-again actions and the new Nick bromance and out-of-character adventures.

Huh. That was quite a list.

"Great. So, how about six thirty? Does that work?" It dawned on me this seemed surprisingly formal for the two of us, but I guess that went with the whole proposing territory.

"Yup. See you at six thirty."

We said quick good-byes and hung up.

Gift, check.

Dinner, check.

Potential groom, check.

See? I was moving right along on the how-to-propose checklist.

I bet Nick would have been helpful in this case.

Now...one last thing. I picked up the phone and dialed, afraid that chaos would suddenly rain down on me.

"Becca Freedman." Becca always answered the phone like that even when I called from my cell which she *definitely* had programmed into her phone.

"Hi, Becca. It's Hailey Tate." Which meant that I had to introduce myself by my full name because...balance.

"Hailey, how are you?" She always sounded so enthusiastic. I was never sure how to take that, but I could sure use some enthusiasm right now. So... Sold!

"I'm great. I have a last-minute sort of thing tonight and I just wanted some suggestions from the binder. Something...something not obvious but special."

"Ohhh that sounds intriguing. I can't wait to see what you guys are up to now."

I took a deep breath. Saying it out loud to Becca seemed like a bigger deal than to Abby. Oddly, I'd known Abby would have my back. But, Becca...

"So, tonight I'm kind of going to have a catered meal for me and Connor at my place and..." More deep breaths. It was totally normal to tell your personal shopper about the intricate and personal details of your life, right? "And, I'm going to propose."

"Propose what?" Becca asked sounding confused and now way less enthusiastic.

"Um, marriage?" I meant it to sound sure and exciting, but doubt was creeping back in.

"Really?" Becca *huh'd* and went on. "Good for you. Why wait around? They never get their butts in gear in time and he's got that training stuff in the spring, right?"

"Yup," I agreed, happy to have her back on board as her enthusiasm level ratcheted back up. "And, he brought up marriage last week and thinking we should get married, so I thought I'd just wrap this up...but, you know, romantically."

"That's great!" She was full-on enthusiasm again. I could hear the faint click-click-click of her heels tapping as she paced her office. "So something pretty and romantic. But nothing that's going to set off warning bells. You want to feel like your best, most confident self, so it has to be very you. And something he'll appreciate and want to hopefully tear off you so, nothing you'll want to wear again."

She went on, talking to me—or more likely herself—describing what sounded like the best thing ever. When she was done pacing and talking, she directed me to the binder.

"Have you worn the dress on page seventy-two?"

Yes, there were more than seventy-two pages in the binder. You can see why it was intimidating.

I flipped to page seventy-two and knew, just knew, she was right.

When I'd opened the garment bag this dress had arrived in,

I'd thought it was the loveliest dress I'd ever owned. Nicer than all the fancy-schmancy event dresses, it was far more me than the other options. I had liked it immediately, I'd then forgotten it in the back of my closet since there wasn't a lot of options for me between yoga pants and Connor's events.

But, there it was. The cashmere fitted dress had cap sleeves and a boatneck cut that both balanced and enhanced my not so need for comfort and desire to look smoking for proposal night.

And yet, at the same time, it didn't feel overdone. It was just a sweet, warm, giant sweater masquerading as a dress.

"This is perfect." I could picture proposing in this. And of course he'd say yes to me in the dress.

"Oh, and, Hailey?" Becca interrupted my thoughts about future love and marital bliss. "Shoes. Don't forget shoes."

Killjoy.

After my call with Becca I cleaned the apartment like it had never been cleaned before, went to the store to make sure I had every possible thing in the kitchen I could ever want, and fielded three calls from Abby—who I was pretty sure was now more nervous than I was.

When I got back from running my errands, Security Dan handed me a package.

"This was delivered from Becca's Beauties." Dan gave me a little grin, a blush shooting up his cheeks.

"So, Dan... Becca, huh?" I asked, wanting love and happiness for everyone in the world.

"I don't know what you're talking about, Hailey, ma'am," he said while not meeting my eyes.

"She works like crazy, is dedicated to her clients, seems a bit obsessive compulsive, has everyone's best interest at heart, and looks amazing in those five-inch heels that might help her clear five-six." I grinned at him as I took the box from his hands. "And, she's perpetually single because of the obsessive compulsive and dedicated things."

Dan nodded, still focusing on a spot over my shoulder.

"I have her number...when you man up."

That finally got his attention. And a glare. I gave him a wink as I took my box and headed for the stairs.

Back in my apartment I opened the box and found a small, gold and pink bag tied shut with a big pink ribbon. Off the ribbon hung a gold tag that read, "My good luck gift to you."

I started to pull the gift from the bag only to realize it was very expensive, very skimpy lingerie. Totally not my thing. I wasn't even sure how the bra went on. I turned it this way and that, realizing it was actually very pretty and more conservative than I'd initially thought. Becca obviously restrained herself for my sensibilities.

And it wasn't polite to let a gift go to waste. I added it to the bed where the sweater dress was laid out.

As the day wore on I paced the apartment, cleaning it again and stalling until it was time to get ready.

The plan was simple: Mac was picking up Connor after a meeting with some potential sponsors who were in town. I was going to go with him, surprising Connor and taking over his evening. He thought he was hanging with Nick, but I'd already canceled those plans. Mac wasn't big on kidnapping Connor on his own so I was here to smooth the way. Also, my absence would let Mr. Antonelli set up our dinner. The watch was already nestled in the oversized pocket of my dress, ready to shock and awe.

As I stood in the middle of my apartment trying to keep excitement at bay, Security Dan rang to let me know Mac was there. I gave my place one last glance and headed out, ready to start the rest of my life.

THIRTY

Mac pulled up to the front of the glass and steel building that stood out between the old walk-ups like the eyesore it was. It matched how I felt about Connor's agent, so there was that.

Connor strolled out of the building, a look of slight annoyance on his face making me want to tell Mac to keep driving. I was pretty sure for me he would—but then Connor would just be annoyed *and* ticked off. Maybe today wasn't proposal day. I glanced at the big building... No day that involved Dex was probably proposal day

He got to the car and jumped in, slumping back in his seat just before he noticed me.

"Hails." He grinned looking like my presence made everything better. "What's going on?"

"Oh, you know, I just thought we could have a nice day together." I smiled at him like that wasn't the lamest thing ever said to anyone anywhere.

"Oh, cool." He took my hand, glancing down at where my

legs stuck out from under my jacket, showing off my low-cut boots and tights. "Are you wearing a dress?"

Of course he sounded confused. When did I ever voluntarily go outside in a dress when it was thirty-four degrees?

"Yup, this is my nice-day-together gear."

"Oh, okay." Connor nodded like this totally made sense.

I think it was the word gear that threw him. Guys and gear, they made sense to one another.

Mac grinned at me in the rearview mirror, staying suspiciously quiet since he was in on the Proposing Plan.

"So, how was Dex today? Coming up with new ways to try to take over the world using your ability to throw a ball and charm the ladies?" I gave him my cocky, ballplayer smile because I knew how much he liked me summarizing his career like that.

"Yeah. And also, after that we're going to create world peace with popsicles."

"Excellent plan."

Connor gave me the side-eye. But humoring his ego only went so far. I typically didn't let it get out of control before it even started.

Before I knew it, we were pulling up in front of my place, and I was both not ready and completely done with waiting. Mac came around and opened the door. Because it was a special occasion night, I let him instead of hopping out as we usually did. At the front of the building, Security Joe had taken over. Security Dan must have clued him in because he winked at me as he held the door open.

I didn't know if the stars were in my favor, but all the guys in my life seemed to be.

We headed up the stairs, Connor chatting away about Dex and casually holding my hand, his thumb rubbing back and forth over it. It was calming...calming...this was good.

This was going to be easy. And romantic. And exactly right. I was going to ask him and he was going to say yes. And this was going to be wonderful.

We got to my door and I fumbled with the key a bit, trying to not rush through one moment. But before I could get it open, Connor's hand covered mine on the doorknob.

"There's something I want to show you," he said, as he pulled me along.

I didn't know where he was going, there wasn't anything above my condo except two more floors. Our roof had never been renovated into a pretty roof deck like so many others in the neighborhood.

I probably shouldn't even think that too loud or Marjory would be charging Connor for that too. So, just the four condos... and nothing.

But we climbed to the top floor and ended up in front of Ms. Jansen's door.

"What's going on?" I asked, wondering where things were going.

"Just wait." He pulled out his keychain and slid a shiny new-looking key into the lock.

"Why do you have Ms. Jansen's key?"

"She moved out, remember?" He gave me the grin. The one he saved for special occasions of charm.

The one he saved for me.

He pushed through the door and held it open, sliding his hand around the corner to hit a light switch. The condo was half-demolished, half-rebuilt. I wasn't sure what was going on. Was Connor moving to my building?

Connor waved me inside and I took in the missing wall where it should have separated this space from the top-floor other condo.

"Where's the wall?" Like that was the most important question.

"Gone." He stood behind me, off to the side, hands in his pocket while I wandered around.

I turned to the left and there was the kitchen he'd been designing. The same pretty granite and understated cabinets.

"Are you moving here?" I asked, unsure how I felt about that.

My space was getting far too small for the two of us, but this seemed extreme. I felt like this was a halfway way to do the next step in our relationship. Not get married, not move in, just take over the entire top floor of my building.

"Maybe."

I walked through the space where the wall should have been and saw the condo had been roughed out differently to give the two spaces flow. There was a master bedroom with an en suite, plus a full bath, and two smaller bedrooms.

The other half had a smaller room and a half-bath. The living area was opened into the dining area then the kitchen. All of it having an open feel, but not so big it felt overwhelming. It all still felt...cozy.

"Maybe? This is a lot of work to *maybe* be moving in here."

"Well." He came around the half drywalled wall I was talking to him through and took my hand. "I'm seriously thinking about moving here, but it would mean a couple things would have to happen first."

"Okay." I had no idea what that meant, but if I knew anything it was not to try to guess what was going on in Connor's head.

Or maybe I could. Gavin was right. We had become *that* couple. The whole night at Gavin's house I could read Connor like a book. Irene, even with all her attention on him, had no idea what was really going on. I doubt Andie and Pete knew the extent that the situation was upsetting him.

Before I knew what was going on, he crossed to me and took my other hand in his.

"I love you, you know that, right?"

"Yes." The same familiar warmth that swept through me every time he said it rushed over me again now. "I love you too."

"I mean, I love you forever. Not for now, or for how we get on together, or for the public couple we are. I'd love you even if you didn't love me. If you left me, in twenty years, I'd still love you. You're it. You're what love is to me."

Oh. Wow.

I could feel the tears sweeping into my eyes, not quite enough to push them out onto my cheeks. But I batted my lashes, pushing them back so I didn't miss anything.

His hand came up to cradle my cheek, and I closed my eyes, letting him make everything be just *so darn right*.

Then the hand disappeared and I opened my eyes to see him drop to one knee. All I could think was *he's getting sawdust on his pants*...because I'm apparently even less sane than I knew.

"Hailey Ann Tate, would you do me that very unquestionable honor of being my wife? I know I'm a bad bet. I know my world and life is as far from what you wanted as possible, but I hope that if I work really hard, I can be worthy of you. That I can make you happy."

"You do make me happy!"

I sniffed, feeling all elegant as my nose ran and tears raced down my cheeks.

"Is that a yes?"

"Yes!" I started to jump into his arms as he rose, and then stopped, stepping back. "Wait, no."

Connor stilled, his hands dropping to his sides.

"No?" he whispered, as I watched the color drain from his face. "No?"

I'd had it all planned out. How was I going to prove to him that I wanted to marry him all the time, that we were soul mates?

What if some day he wondered if I'd only wanted to be with him because he was him?

"I..." Oh my gosh, my plan was going right out the window. I reached in my pocket and wrapped my hand around the watch safely stowed there. "I want to marry you."

Connor looked just as worried, but also confused now. "Okayyyyyy," he drew the word out.

"I mean, of course I do." I gave him my most reassuring smile.

"Great, so... Yes?"

"No."

"No?"

"Well, yes...I mean no, but in a no-but-yes kind of way."

Connor ran his hand through his hair, tussling it out of place. When it didn't fall back to where it usually lay lovely and shiny, I knew he was thrown more out of whack than I could measure.

"Hailey..." He drawled out my name like I was killing him. "You're killing me."

Okay.

"So—" I glanced around knowing that I had to adjust my plan, trying to make this work without my fancy dinner and candlelight. I glanced down and I was still wearing my coat! "I want to do this right."

Connor scowled and glanced around, his gaze going off to the distance as he nodded his head like he was counting things.

"I'm not sure what I missed. Did I skip something?" I could all but see him struggling not to call Nick to ask for a proposal checklist.

"No! That was the best proposal ever!" I still had tears in my eyes.

"But..." He scowled some more. "You didn't say yes so it couldn't have been that great... Also, how many proposals have you gotten?"

"Just the one."

"This one?"

"Of course, this one!"

Connor stepped back a bit. "Well, I just wanted to make sure. So then what are you comparing it to?" He glanced away before adding, "It just sounds like you've been running around town, turning down proposals."

"No." Now I scowled. We were way off track here. "But that rivaled even my favorite romance novels. It was wonderful. You made me feel really loved."

"Oh, well. Thank you." Connor nodded as if this helped. "So then, yes?"

I tried not to scowl again since it was beginning to feel like there was a lot of scowling going on in this proposal of marriage.

"So, can I ask?" I gave him my best smile.

Connor looked at me as if I were a crazy woman who had taken over his girlfriend's body. That wasn't too weird since I'd been feeling that way lately too.

"Sure, Hails. Ask me anything." He gave me his most reassuring smile. The one when he wasn't trying to charm or cajole, but when he was really there. Smiling at you, loving you. Obviously, he was trying to get this moved along.

"Okay." I reached into the dress pocket and wrapped my hand around the watch. "Connor Ryan, you are by far the most wonderful, clever, kind, exasperating man I've ever known...ever even known of. I love you with all my heart. Will you do me the very great honor of marrying me?"

I pulled the watch out of my pocket, still wrapped and hidden in my hand, when Connor's smile faded to a very confused look.

"But, I just asked you and you said no."

"No, I said no-but-yes. Well, I said yes, then no, then no-but-yes."

"So, why don't you just say yes?"

"Because I asked you."

"I asked you first."

I stared at him, struggling to come up with an alternative reason. But he did have a point. He asked first.

"Hails, this is probably the most ridiculous conversation I've ever had...and that includes everything with Gavin ever."

I glanced down at the watch wrapped in my hand and the box barely peeking out of his.

"Wait...did you get me a ring?" He sounded both annoyed and intrigued.

"No."

"No?"

"No."

"So, what's that thing in your hand?"

I stuck my hand behind my back. "You didn't say yes."

"Well, maybe I'd say yes if I knew what I was getting out of it."

"Me! You're getting me!"

"And, sweetheart, you know—since I already proposed to you and you said yes-no-no-but-yes—that I want you. But now that there's a gift involved I want to see my options."

"Your options are: me... Then you get a gift."

"Hmmm..." Connor stroked his chin like an evil villain over-lord thinking over a high-level negotiation. This was probably what Dex looked like in their meetings.

"You know what?" I slipped the watch back in my pocket. "That's okay. I'll just marry you. You don't have to marry me."

"Well, maybe I'm rescinding my offer. Maybe I'm more inter-ested in your offer now."

I glared at him, wondering how I could play this out. I wanted to marry him, but if he was rescinding his proposal...that wasn't a very good start to a marriage. I didn't want to be a proposal bully.

Connor glanced around the condo, looking even more frustrated than I felt.

"What if, we both accepted the other's proposal at the same time? That seems very pro-union, right?" He looked at me like this was a genius idea.

Of course I didn't have anything better in mind, so sure. I nodded, not knowing how this was going to work.

But, as soon as I did, his shoulders dropped back down to where they usually lived.

"Okay, on the count of three, we both say yes."

"Wait— like one, two, yes? Or one, two, three, yes?"

"One, two, yes."

Connor started to count and it dawned on me he'd probably not say yes so he could be the man proposing. So when he got to three, I said nothing.

And he said, "Yes!" then, "Hailey."

He said yes. He said *yes*.

I dove at him, so excited, thrilled to be engaged to this man I loved so much.

"Yes! Of course, it's a yes!"

Because after this last month, after the challenges and overthinking and the wonderful talk with Gavin, it could never be anything other than a yes.

He grinned, a dopey grin I knew I was one of the few people who ever got to see it. "Yes, right? Yes?"

I nodded again, so happy, so overjoyed.

Connor pulled me to him, softly like I was a fragile gift, and lowered his head, brushing his lips across mine.

"Mine. My Hailey Ann for always."

I melted against him, knowing the only place that would ever be home was with this man. This man who couldn't be held back or tacked down to one place. I'd spend my life watching him running circles around the rest of the world and resting safely in the eye of his storm where he'd always return to me.

He deepened the kiss, pulling me tight against him, making me realize that even if I'd ever wanted to get away from him, it never would have happened because he knew as well as I did that we were two halves of a whole.

After he pulled away and placed a tasteful, normal-sized ring on my normal-sized hand, he rocked back on his heels.

"Well?"

"Well, what?"

"What did you propose to me with?"

"Oh, nothing." I grinned and glanced around, pretending to be distracted by the condo.

"Really?" He drew out the word and I knew he wasn't going to let it go.

"So, I wanted to get you something that wasn't a ring. Something you could keep and have on you when you have a special occasion. Something solid—as solid as us—that you could hold in your hand." I pulled the watch out of my pocket, holding it out in front of us from where I was tucked under Connor's arm. "And this, seemed perfect."

"Oh, wow. Hails." He held his hand out to touch it where it rest in my palm, his shaking just a bit.

I explained about the Celtic Shield Knot and how it would keep him safe while he traveled and showed that he was bound to me. That we were bound together. When I looked up, his gaze was locked on it, a tear running down his cheek as he turned that gaze on me.

"You are the absolute best thing that has ever happened to me. That *will* ever happen to me. I don't know how I became so blessed, but I feel it here." He tapped his free hand over his heart. "I feel that knot binding us here."

We stood there, just us being us, for a moment.

Then, I realized where I was.

"So," I asked, snuggling deeper into the place he'd tucked me under his arm like he'd never let me go. "What's up with this condo?"

"Oh." He suddenly looked disappointed, like he'd messed something up. "This was part of my proposal, but..."

"But what?" Because this was a really weird thing to overlook.

The pink raced over his cheeks, looking like a kid caught doing something he'd explicitly been told not to. "I got nervous."

Mr. Big Shot Baseball Star got nervous?

Before I could ask about that, he rushed me around showing me the details we'd been picking out over the last month. Including my office, off to the side, far away from the guest rooms, where I could go and hide out.

"I love being here and I know you do too, but there was no way we could live in your place." He looked apologetic, like he was stating something I didn't know was true. "I figured I'd grab this chance to make a penthouse and hope that it worked for you. That being here would make you happy. You could totally keep your place and use it as an office if you want. You don't have to use the office up here."

"And this was part of the proposal?"

"Well, yeah." He looked at me as if it should be obvious.

I tried to wait him out, tried to figure out how this could have been part of that already perfect proposal. I finally said, "I'm sorry, Connor, I don't know how it fits."

"Oh." He glanced around then took my hand over to the window where we could just see the park one block over, the lights of the city a soft flicker around us. "Well, I thought about what marriage was and the things I would be swearing to. To love, honor, and cherish you. I can do that. I do that now. That's how I feel, but a man is also supposed to provide."

He put up a hand stopping me before I could say anything about the ridiculousness of that.

"Wait. Because, I know. I know you can provide for yourself. You'll never *need* anything. But the thing I can provide is your happiness. You love it here and if I could do anything to keep you somewhere you were happy, I wanted to make sure we could make it happen."

I glanced around, realizing he'd built us a little corner of heaven. A place where happiness had a home.

A place where two worlds really could become one. I was home.

EPILOGUE

I got to The Brew at about six, knowing forcing Abby to open early twice in one month was just asking for undercooked brownies.

I'd texted the girls, asking them to meet me for an early breakfast...not quite calling it an emergency, but at this hour what else could they think?

I was mostly thrilled—but I'm not gonna lie, I was also scared to death that this meeting was going to go like the one at the beginning of the month.

I walked up to the counter, waiting in line behind the super early commuters getting their morning fix.

Abby paused when she saw me, looking thoughtful but not surprised. At least I didn't look like I was going to break down this time...and the fire was already going, so I was off the hook there.

I got to the counter and ordered, like that was necessary. Instead of paying attention, Abby glanced down at my left hand where the ring sat tastefully on my finger, not overwhelming or absurd. But a ring to match me. A ring I loved, not one that announced how much money my boyfriend—*fiancé*—had.

She smiled, one of her rare, true smiles and said, "Good," before handing me my tea and shooing me along.

The girls got to The Brew, each one giving me a look as she went to the counter and ordered before joining me in our comfy seats.

I made sure to keep my left hand tucked safely away while I waited for a lull in the commuter coffee addicts. Once Abby joined us, I started working up the nerve to try again. Hoping beyond hope that it went smoother this time.

Connor, being overly aware of me, had already realized I was nervous to tell the girls and I ended up spilling some of the things that had been going on.

"Hails, *of course* they'd worry. They love you." He'd given me a tight squeeze and left it at that.

If anything could have made me fall more in love with him, he'd pretty much nailed it.

Abby collapsed into the chair across from me looking smug and proud of herself. You'd think Connor and I had been an arranged marriage she'd negotiated herself.

Now that we were all there, I kept putting it off. I could tell the girls were all chatting and waiting for me to say something. The last time I'd texted them this early, I'd been a mess. I hadn't known if I had good news or a disaster on my hands.

I was nothing but happy and trying to squash my own glow for fear of letting them squash it instead.

Finally, Abby jerked her head toward the others, a clear sign it was time to get a move on. She had muffins to make after all.

"So," I started, unsure how to say everything I was thinking while telling them that Connor had proposed *and* that I'd said yes. Instead, I just pulled my hand out from where it had hid up my sleeve and showed them the beautiful ring that said the man I loved was mine to keep.

There was stunned silence and then…Jenna burst into tears.

Sobbing, body-wracking tears.

We all sat there, shocked. A stillness settling over the group in a way I don't think I'd ever witnessed before.

The front door started to open, and Abby jumped up. "Sorry! We're closed."

The man started to argue that all he wanted was coffee and she shook her head, pointing toward the door before crossing and locking it behind him.

"Jenna?" I asked, afraid of where this was going, afraid I was going to have to pick between people I loved.

"I'm so…" she sucked in a breath, "I'm so *happy*."

"You are?"

"I am!" She jumped up and leapt across the table. "You were so right. And I've been stupid. I'm so glad we talked about it. He really does love you and I want that for you so much. You deserve to be loved like that!"

Jenna wrapped her arms around me, sobbing even harder.

I patted her on the back, taken aback by how this had turned out. Over her shoulder, Kasey and Jayne looked pleased, Kasey flashing me a thumbs-up. Abby still looked smug.

Once Jenna stopped crying, she shuffled back to her seat and collapsed into it like she'd just fought a war.

"I was so afraid I ruined things. Either with you guys or us. But it's okay, right? Everything's good?"

"Everything is great." And it was.

Jayne lavished her love of the artistic design of my ring, Kasey commented on Connor's choice as classic good taste.

And Abby just kept looking smug.

We talked about the fact that spring training was coming up so we had a short window to get married if it was going to be before the holidays next December. And what kind of wedding I wanted. And the new condo. Which everyone looked surprised about.

Except Abby.

She just continued looking smug.

John finally showed up, coming through the locked front door and looking at Abby like she was insane for closing the shop right as commuter hours were starting. But once he heard what was going on, he was all good.

I mean, who could argue with my girls? Especially when Jenna flashed him smile number five and said, "And they'll live happily ever after."

EXCERPT: WORTH THE FALL (BREW HA HA #2)

CHAPTER ONE

"You're dumping me?"

I could *not* believe this was happening. Every time. Every time I thought this week couldn't get worse—BAM! It did.

"Come on, Kasey. You can't be shocked by this." Jason looked at me over the very nice, very expensive dinner he'd invited me to, pity shining through those narrowed eyes.

I sucked in a deep breath, glancing away to focus because this just didn't make sense.

"You're really doing this tonight? Seriously?" At the moment, I was more shocked than heartbroken. Although, as I pondered it, heartbreak would probably attack as soon as I was home alone in my apartment...my very, *very* empty apartment.

I'd have to sit on the floor to have a good cry.

"I'm sorry you're so surprised," Jason said, although he didn't sound the least bit sorry.

"Surprised? I was supposed to move in with you this weekend."

He tipped his head to the side and looked at me like he might be humoring a child. "You can't really move in now, right?"

"Well, not if you're breaking up with me I can't, can I?" My voice shot up. It sounded a bit hysterical even to my own ears. In the back of my mind, I realized people were beginning to look our way. Jason was going to hate that.

He reached across the table and wrapped his hand around mine, giving it a harsh squeeze. Even his fake comfort was...well, fake.

"If you moved, how were you going to pay your half of the rent? How would you be able to carry your weight?"

Carry my weight? We'd been dating for almost three years and now he was dumping me because I might not be able to pay rent for a couple months on a condo he already owned?

"Give me a break, Jason. I lost my freaking job yesterday. Do you think I have nothing in the bank? You pick the day after I got laid-off to do this?" The hysteria was gone. In its place my emotional cup was filled to the brim with near-blinding rage.

"The economy is tight." He shrugged as if none of this really mattered. "Who's to say you'll find something right away?"

I could not believe this. Could. Not. Believe it. Just last week we'd finished selling all my furniture on Craigslist because his already "fit" in his place. I'd canceled my lease, paid the fine to break it, and was homeless as of the end of the month—which conveniently happened in two days.

"Here." He handed me a card.

A card. I looked at the lavender sealed envelope. Was I supposed to open it? Did Hallmark really make an I'm-Dumping-Your-Ass-But-Good-Luck-With-Everything card?

"What's this?"

"That's the first month's rent and half of the security you'd paid. I figured it was only fair to give it back."

You think? I looked down at the card again, wondering what he'd written in it, tempted to open it right then. In retrospect, giving him the security deposit should have been the first sign.

Okay, maybe not the first.

"So, where exactly do you think I'm going to live?"

Scorn. I'd moved from rage to scorn. I was now officially a woman scorned.

No wonder men weren't supposed to cross us. If hell had no fury like me at that moment, it still had a lot of leash to run on. I could have gutted him with the fancy fish knife resting against my plate.

"Well, I don't want to sound heartless," Jason continued studying his plate before looking up with the least empathetic expression I'd ever seen, "but that's not really my problem now, is it?"

The woman at the next table gasped and that's when I realized most of the tables had fallen silent to the melodrama playing out that was my life.

"No. I guess not. I guess when you dump your girlfriend because she lost her job, you think just about nothing is your problem." I pushed my chair out, wrapped myself in my Ann Taylor jacket, and picked up my purse. "Oh, wait. You know what your problem is?"

He shook his head, a small smirk yanking his mouth up into cruel tips on each side.

"Getting Bordeaux out of cashmere." I picked up our half empty bottle of wine and dumped it out on his head. "Good luck with that."

I stormed away, a smattering of applause following me in my wake. Angry tears nearly blinded me by the time I reached the lobby.

"Please. Allow me." The host pushed the door open and held

it for me as I marched into the cool, spring night. "Good luck, miss."

Yeah. I was going to need it.

KEEP READING *Worth the Fall*

ABOUT BRIA

Quirky Girl and all around lovable klutz, Bria Quinlan writes Diet-Coke-Snort-Worthy Rom Coms about what it's like to be a girl and deal with crap and still look for love.

She also writes books for teens that take hard topics and make you laugh through your tears...or maybe cry through your laughter. Some people call them issue books. Some people call them romantic comedies. Bria calls them what-life-looks-like.

Her stories remind you that life is an adventure not to be ignored.

If these things are important to you: she's a RWA RITA, Golden Heart, & Cyblis nominee as well as a USA Today Best Seller, and natural blonde represented by the awesomely amazing Laird Lauren Macleod of the Clan.... Oh, wait. Of Strothman Agency.

Want to hangout? Check her out here:
briaquinlan.com/

Made in the USA
Lexington, KY
15 November 2017